It All Started with
Autumn Jones

It All Started with Autumn Jones

a novel

JACK WEYLAND

DESERET
BOOK

SALT LAKE CITY, UTAH

"Infinite Monkey Theorem" described on pages 35–36 can be found online at en.wikipedia.org/wiki/Infinite_monkey_theorem.

Quote from "The Family: A Proclamation to the World" on page 37 from *Ensign,* November 1995, 102.

Quote from Boyd K. Packer on pages 74–75 from *Memorable Stories and Parables by Boyd K. Packer* (Salt Lake City: Bookcraft, 1997), 73–76.

Quote from Gordon B. Hinckley on page 82 from "U.S. Conference of Mayors," *Ensign,* November 1998, 109.

© 2010 Jack Weyland

Visit us at DeseretBook.com

Library of Congress Cataloging-in-Publication Data

Weyland, Jack, 1940–

    It all started with Autumn Jones / Jack Weyland.

        p. cm.

    Summary: When Nick Baxter has to choose whether or not to stand up for his religious beliefs against his college professor, he risks losing his chance to get into law school. But he just might win the heart of the girl of his dreams.

    ISBN 978-1-60641-840-6 (pbk.)

    1. Law students—Fiction.   2. Mormons—Fiction.   3. Dating (Social customs)—Fiction.
I. Title.

    PS3573.E99I8 2010

    813'.54—dc22   2010019684

Printed in the United States of America
Worzalla Publishing Company, Stevens Point, WI

10   9   8   7   6   5   4   3   2   1

Chapter One

All I wanted from my Contemporary Issues class was to escape being singled out by its professor, Dr. T. Penstock, known by anyone who'd ever taken the class as "Thomas the Terrible."

My plan to avoid detection was simple: ask no questions, raise no issues, and stay in the background.

I'd have done it too, if it weren't for the coming of Autumn.

Oh, not the season. The girl.

• • •

I went early the first day of class in order to choose a strategically safe seat. Students who had taken the class before warned the new students not to sit in the first three rows. Penstock would see the fear in your eyes, and that's all he'd need to make your life miserable. The back row wasn't safe either because Penstock knew that's where all the slackers sat.

I chose a seat in the center behind a guy so large he could get a job temping for Mount Rushmore. Privately, I called him Godzilla. By sitting behind him, I'd be hidden from Penstock's view.

Godzilla smelled of strong cologne. I wondered if his dad gave it to him to make him more popular with the girls. Actually, his dad should've just told him to take more showers, because, as I soon discovered, the cologne was fighting an uphill battle.

It was a cold, dreary Monday in January, the first day of winter semester at the prestigious Gresham University, about twenty miles from Chicago. It was my last semester before graduation.

Precisely at ten o'clock, Penstock entered the classroom, trailed by three graduate student clones wearing white lab jackets. Two of them took their places at the doors. Several students who arrived late to class were turned away by the graduate goons guarding the doors.

"First rule!" Penstock thundered. "Be early or go home!"

The third graduate student, whose first language was obviously not English, took roll. He managed to mispronounce every name—even Smith and Jones.

As roll was being taken, Penstock paced up and down the aisles like a lion looking for an easy kill. I'd been told the worst thing to do when Penstock was on the prowl was to duck down to avoid being noticed. If you did that, he'd be sure to turn on you.

I'd also heard not to fix your gaze on him. But don't *not* look at him either.

Also, no cell phones. Legend had it that Penstock once threw a student's Blackberry against the wall because he caught him texting.

Armed with the knowledge of how to avoid Penstock's first-day feeding frenzy, I'd come up with what I hoped was a foolproof plan: I'd let him catch me reading the textbook and be at least on page 20. As he passed, I'd glance up at him momentarily and go back to reading, like I couldn't get enough of the stuff.

That's what I did, and it worked. He passed by me on his way to harass some guy on the back row who was wearing a Chicago White Sox hat. He yanked the hat off the student's head and handed it to one of his graduate students, who held it by the brim like it was a dirty sock.

"No hats in class!" Penstock roared.

With roll taken and all of us properly on edge, it was time for Penstock to get serious. From what I'd been told by previous students, Penstock always spent the first day of class making progressively more radical statements to see if anyone would challenge his position on an issue. If someone did, he'd make that person his "whipping boy" for the semester.

I learned early on that this was not going to be a class where both sides of an issue would be presented. Penstock's goal was to convert another group of Gresham University's finest to his radically liberal point of view.

Fifteen minutes into his lecture, just after Penstock had stated that anyone who believed in God was an idiot, a girl raised her hand.

Penstock continued his rant until she stood up and in a

3

bold voice said, "Dr. Penstock, with all due respect, I do not happen to agree with you."

Penstock got a sick and twisted grin on his face. "And what do you have to sustain your position?"

She paused. "Me, personally?" Much to my surprise, she took out her quad and began to read, "'All things denote there is a God; yea, even the earth, and all things that are upon the face of it, yea, and its motion, yea—'"

I wondered if she were a singer because her voice carried so well.

"Young woman, may I remind you that this is a university," Penstock began in a sort of singsong voice. He then added in a thunderous denouncement, "I do not allow mumbo jumbo Bible passages to be read in this class!"

I was surprised when the girl didn't back down. "I take it then that you do not believe the Bible to be the word of God," she stated.

"I most certainly do not."

She shrugged. "Fair enough." She continued reading from the same page, "'And also all the planets which move in their regular form do witness that there is a Supreme Creator.'"

Penstock barely controlled his anger. "What did I just tell you?"

"That you don't want Bible passages read out loud in class."

"That's right. So why are you still reading?"

"Well, actually, Dr. Penstock, this is from the Book of Mormon, which, of course, is not the Bible."

Clearly not used to such insubordination, Penstock looked as though he might have a stroke. He said in a menacing voice, "Young lady, let me put this to you very simply. I do not want you to ever again read out loud from either the Book of Mormon or the Bible in this class."

"Understood," she replied, but instead of sitting down, she turned a few pages and began to read again. "'The light and the Redeemer of the world, the Spirit of truth, who came into the world, because the world was made by him—'"

"Young lady, your continued enrollment in this class is in serious jeopardy."

"But this is from the Doctrine and Covenants. It contains revelations from Jesus Christ to the Prophet Joseph Smith."

I was in awe, and the rest of the students were too. We sat in uneasy silence. Watching this debate was like watching a train wreck. I admired her boldness, but I was also afraid for her. Hadn't anyone warned her about Penstock? Or was she baiting him on purpose?

He looked like he'd reached the end of his patience. "Let me make this clear. I do not want you to read anything from any book that claims to have come from God."

"Dr. Penstock, with all due respect, have you ever read the Bible?"

"No."

"The Book of Mormon?"

"Certainly not."

"The Doctrine and Covenants?"

"No."

"How about *Mere Christianity* by C. S. Lewis?"

"No."

She got a silly grin on her face. "How about *The Lion, the Witch, and the Wardrobe,* also by C. S. Lewis?"

One or two students laughed, but Penstock's legendary Glare of Doom immediately wiped the smiles off their faces.

"Young woman, you are wasting the time of the rational students in this class," Penstock declared.

"Let me find out if that's true." She turned to the class. "Is there anyone here who will support me in my position that something other than random chance brought this world and everything in it into being?"

None of us, including me, raised a hand.

"And what does that tell you?" Penstock asked the girl sarcastically.

"It tells me that you've already intimidated everyone in the class except me." She addressed the class. "If some of you don't step up to the plate, we're going to spend the semester being indoctrinated into Dr. Penstock's version of reality. That's not why I took this class. How about you?"

Nobody moved a muscle.

She shook her head. "Well, if any of you change your mind, please let me or Dr. Penstock know."

I actually agreed with her and felt awful because I'd just sat there like everyone else.

"Young woman—"

"My name is Autumn Jones. Oh, also, it's not pronounced Joan-ease as your assistant said when he took roll."

"Ms. Jones, I'm curious—where did you learn to stand up for what you believe?" he asked with something that sounded like a mixture of disdain and respect.

"I served a full-time mission for The Church of Jesus Christ of Latter-day Saints. I served in New York City where for a year and a half I spent every day explaining to people what I believe—people I met on subways and on the street, as well as esteemed professors such as yourself. Because I knew that what I was teaching was true, I learned not to apologize for my faith. That's why I am the way I am today."

"Let that be a warning to the rest of you," Penstock said with a grim smile.

She smiled back. "Also, my dad is the mayor of a small town."

"What town?" Penstock asked.

"Scottsburg. My dad always stands up for what he believes is the right course of action for the town. Nobody gets more grief than a mayor. He's gotten used to it, and I guess I have too."

"If you'll sit down, perhaps we can continue."

"Yes, of course. Thank you for letting me speak." She sat down.

Dr. Penstock picked a different topic and continued.

While he talked, I kept looking at her. She was amazing; she didn't seem the least bit embarrassed or even flustered. Man, what a show of courage. I'd served a mission too. I should have at least raised my hand when she asked if there was anyone who agreed with her. I should have said something. But I hadn't. And, the truth was, I probably never would.

Part of the reason I felt I had to remain silent in class was because I'd been such a slacker during my freshman year. I didn't go to class much or study, and I ended up with a 0.7 grade point average. After my mission, I'd worked hard and had eventually raised my overall grade point average to a 3.1—good enough to graduate, but not good enough to be accepted into Harvard Law School, where my dad had attended—and where I wanted to go.

7

When my dad had been a student, he'd roomed with a guy who was now the dean of Harvard Law School. When Dad called him about me, the dean said that if I got all As my last semester at Gresham, they'd accept me on a provisional basis in the fall.

The plan was that once I got a law degree, I'd start working for my dad in his law firm.

My other classes at Gresham this semester were going to be easy, so my entire future depended on this class. I needed an A from Penstock.

Students who'd taken his class before had told me that if you wanted an A, all you had to do was act as though you agreed with Penstock during his lectures, say something once in a while in class, and write a term paper that essentially agreed with everything he believed. The class syllabus itself said there were only three components in earning a high grade:

1. Attendance. (Penstock was a stickler on this one. Rule number one: be in class!)
2. Participation in class discussions. (You had to speak up, but it helped if you agreed with his point of view.)
3. Write a single, cogent, twenty-page term paper on an approved topic. (Approved by the tyrant himself.)

I rationalized: *If I stand up for what I believe, then I won't get an A in this class, which means I won't be accepted into Harvard. I can always defend truth after I'm a partner in Dad's law firm.*

While Penstock rambled on and on about something, I focused my attention on Autumn Jones. She wasn't bad-looking. Her brown hair was pulled back into a ponytail, like she had more important things to do than spend time on her hair. She had large brown eyes. She didn't seem to be wearing much makeup, and I thought it would have helped her appearance. I guessed that she was about five-foot-nine.

Autumn was wearing charcoal-gray pants, a cream-colored shirt buttoned to the top, and an expensive-looking, long-sleeved, raspberry-colored sweater. My problem was that she looked like someone who'd served a mission.

She was also wearing glasses. They made her look, well, too intelligent. That kind of girl never appealed to me.

I was trying to imagine how much better she'd look with contacts when I noticed her bow her head and close her eyes.

She's praying? I thought. I shook my head. *Your mission is over, girl. It's time to move on. Like I have, for example.*

I felt sorry for her. She must be one of those missionaries who have a hard time making the transition after they get home. *She's probably praying for divine guidance. But she's not going to get it here. Who in this class is ever going to give her any help?*

Have you ever had a thought come into your mind that seems to come from somewhere outside of yourself? Well, that happened to me then, and the thought was simple: *You need to help her.*

Not me, I thought. *If I go against Dr. Penstock, I'll never get the A I need in this class.*

Do it anyway.

It was like the feeling you get when you know you need to bear your testimony. As much as I tried, I couldn't make the impression go away. I felt hot, and I was having a hard time breathing.

Finally I gave a big sigh and raised my hand, thinking, *This is going to be a disaster.*

"Yes?" Penstock asked irritably.

"I agree with Autumn Jones."

"How so?" he queried.

I could feel a line of sweat running down my side as I said, "You know, with what she said."

Penstock fixed his steely glare on me. "What's your name?"

Before my mission, I'd been known as Nick, but this environment seemed to require more formality. "Nicolas Baxter," I said.

"And do you believe in God, too, Mr. Baxter?"

"Yes, sir, I do."

"What specific point would you like to make?"

"Uh, specific point?" I stammered.

"Yes, that's what we do in our discussions in this class. Make specific points."

"Actually, I haven't seen much discussion here so far," I said without thinking.

"That's because everyone agrees with my position. Except you and your naïve friend here."

Autumn and I traded glances. "Oh, hi there," I said, feeling stupid.

She gave me an anemic wave and a faint smile.

"Do you have any rational statement you'd like to make?" Penstock asked. "Or is that asking too much of you and Ms. Jones?"

I took a deep breath and began. "Just one comment, if I may. In the syllabus it says you encourage free and open discussion. That must mean you realize not everyone will agree with you. But the word from past students is that you only give As to those who parrot back your point of view. Is that true?"

"I grade students based on the merit of their arguments."

Being the son of a lawyer had some benefits. "With all due respect, sir, can you give me an idea of what would constitute a good argument? Would it ever be one that opposed your position, for example?"

I could tell Penstock was getting annoyed with me. "What are you saying?"

"I just want to know if it is possible to disagree with you and still get an A in this class. Or will I have to keep my personal opinions and beliefs to myself? Apparently everyone here has already decided to stay quiet. They must have gone online like I did and read what past students have said about you as a teacher. By the way, have you ever read those reviews? Man, that's got to be a real downer for you, right?"

Not surprisingly, he gave me his Glare of Doom. "As the syllabus says, I encourage free and open discussion," he insisted.

"Well, that's great, sir, because that's what you're going to get from Autumn and me."

"You're both idiots then. Sit down and let me continue."

But I didn't sit down. "Excuse me. Just one more question. Are you saying we're idiots just because we don't agree with you?"

"No, I'm saying you're idiots because you have done nothing to present a cogent argument."

"With all due respect, sir, neither have you."

I noticed Autumn cringe. Maybe I'd gone too far.

That set Penstock off. Pointing to the door, he yelled,

"That's it! I've had it. Mr. Baxter, get out of this classroom and don't ever come back!"

I stood my ground. "No, sir, I will not! I think what's happening here is what might possibly be characterized as a 'free and open discussion,' which you so eloquently invite in your syllabus, and which, by the way, is guaranteed by the Constitution." I tapped my forehead. "Oh, sorry! You have heard of the Constitution of the United States, right?"

Okay, I admit that might have been just a little over the top.

Penstock was beyond furious at me. He pulled his cell phone from his briefcase. "That's it! I'll have you arrested for disturbing the peace!"

"Arrested?" I asked. "You can't be serious!"

"You just watch and see if I'm serious!"

Autumn made her way out of her row and over to where I was standing in the aisle. "If you're going to have Nicolas arrested for merely expressing his opinion, then you'll have to arrest me too."

"That, Ms. Jones, will be a pleasure."

I'd had it with him. "Before we're hauled away to jail, Dr. Penstock, I have just one suggestion. I think you might want to change the name of this course to 'Liberal Indoctrination.'"

As Penstock was punching in the number for campus security, Autumn started laughing. Both Penstock and I stared at her.

"What is so amusing, Ms. Jones?" Penstock fumed.

"I was just thinking how this is going to look on Fox News! Bill O'Reilly is going to have so much fun with this!"

I leaned over and said quietly to her, "Ouch!"

She nodded.

Penstock called security anyway and demanded they come and remove two unruly students.

While he was on the phone, Autumn asked Godzilla if he'd be willing to use her cell phone to record us being escorted out of class by campus security.

"Yeah, sure," he said. "No problem." He stood up alongside us. Autumn handed him her cell and made arrangements to pick it up before one of his classes later that day.

"When they take us away, try to get both us and the security cops in the same frame," Autumn instructed Godzilla, speaking loud enough for Penstock to hear.

"You really think this will be on Fox News?" Godzilla said.

"Absolutely! Probably every day for at least a week. We'll make sure to give you full credit for your help too."

Autumn asked him what his name was and where he was from. Unlike me, she didn't seem to be bothered by his body odor.

By the time campus security showed up, Penstock had cooled down enough to become rational. He told them there was no problem after all and that they could leave. Then he turned and wrote our reading assignment for next class on the blackboard before storming out the faculty access door, slamming it shut.

Autumn retrieved her cell phone from Godzilla on his way out. Everyone quickly escaped the classroom, except for Autumn and me. Most of the class members looked at me like I was crazy, and one guy said to me as he walked by, "Nice start, dude."

I shook my head. What had I just done?

Chapter Two

While Autumn returned to her seat and gathered her things, I waited for her at the classroom door.

"So, anything interesting happen during your first day of class?" I teased as we walked out into the hall.

She got a big grin on her face. "Not really. Same old, same old."

"You want to get something to eat?" I asked. "My treat."

"Yeah, sure."

We headed for the student union. "This is a little awkward, isn't it?" I said.

"In what way?"

"We don't know each other, and yet, here we are, thrown together by forces totally beyond our control," I said.

She laughed. "That sounds like a movie teaser."

I took the bait. In a movie-trailer voice, I announced, "Two strangers—thrown together by cosmic forces totally beyond their control!" I also added dialogue. "So, Penstock, we meet again! But this time *I* will be victorious!"

It felt great to make her laugh.

"I suppose in your male fantasy imagination, you probably think you rescued me today, right?" she teased.

"Yeah, pretty much. Does it make you mad that I'd think that?"

"Not really. I know how it is with guys. On my mission, when anything good happened in our area, our district and zone leaders took credit for it. Any setback we had was totally our fault."

After a long pause, I said softly, "Oh."

She tapped her forehead with her hand. "Let me guess. You were a mission leader, weren't you?"

"Maybe."

"What were you? Mission assistant? Zone leader? You're dying to tell me, aren't you? I promise I'll be properly impressed."

"I was in charge of the cars."

"I bet that wasn't easy, was it?"

"No, not at all. Most people figure it's not that important. But, you know what? The Church has a lot of money invested in a mission fleet of cars. They need to be properly maintained."

"Of course they do. Your mission president must have been very grateful for the work you did."

Nothing she could have said would have won me over more. Some missionaries thought the only reason I was asked to be in charge of the mission fleet was because I was some kind of problem elder who needed to be under the thumb of the mission president. That, of course, was not the case.

I bought a sandwich, and we split it.

"Do you have time now to prepare for our next class with Penstock?" she asked.

"Yeah, I've got a couple of hours before my next class."

"There's a great place in the library where we'll be able to discuss strategies for our class without disturbing anyone."

Once we reached the library, she led me to an elevator. She punched the button for the third floor. The elevator door opened, revealing a huge room with eight vacant desks. She led me past the desks to another door with a sign that read "Conference Room—By Appointment Only." Next to the door was a sign-up sheet on a desk. The last time anyone other than Autumn had signed up for the conference room had been over a year ago.

She signed us in, grabbed a key from a drawer below the sign-up sheet, unlocked the door, and we stepped into what I could only describe as student heaven.

A long, mahogany conference table surrounded by expensive leather chairs filled the middle of the room. In front of the table was a large sofa facing a large, natural-stone fireplace that probably had not been used for years. A built-in bookcase with four shelves filled with expensive-looking books covered another wall. On one of the other walls was a large picture of C. Gregory Gresham, the benefactor who had donated the money necessary to found the university more than a century earlier. On the last wall there was a refrigerator, a microwave, and a water fountain.

"Make yourself at home," she said. "Soft drinks are in the refrigerator. Just put fifty cents in the box on the counter when you take one."

"Only fifty cents?"

"That's what it says."

I grabbed two Sprites and dropped a dollar in the small cardboard box. I handed a can to Autumn, then plopped down on the sofa and looked around. "This is amazing! How did you ever find this place?" I asked.

"I got lost looking for a book and ended up here. Any time I don't have a class I come here. You could do the same thing. That way we could optimize our time working together."

"I'm all for optimizing our time together," I said with a stupid grin that must have set off major alarm bells for her because she blushed and looked away.

"Okay. Just one thing. Occasionally library staff members come in here, so it's not like we're totally alone. I mean, it wouldn't be appropriate, you know, for us to be alone . . . here. I don't want you to think I brought you here just so we could be alone."

"Never crossed my mind," I said with all the fake sincerity I possessed.

She seemed relieved. "Good. Just so we understand each other. This will primarily be a working relationship. Oh, one other thing. I'm waiting for a missionary. I just thought you should know at the outset."

"When does he get home?"

"Near the end of April."

I would graduate the middle of May. "No problem. Well, should we get to work?"

"Sounds good."

We sat across from each other at the conference table. We reviewed the assigned pages in the textbook. Then, based on the reading, we tried to guess what direction Dr. Penstock's lecture would go.

We divided up the research we'd need to do to prepare for those topics and then agreed to meet back the next day to make sure we were prepared for class on Wednesday. Our class met every Monday, Wednesday, and Friday, and we figured out we could meet both before and after class.

That night Autumn texted me with questions and comments from the reading assignment. I gave her my thoughts on what she'd written, but then I made the mistake of asking her if she liked to dance. She texted back that she had to go. I felt like an idiot for even asking her about dancing when I knew she was waiting for a missionary.

On my walk to campus the next day, I passed a store called Chocolate Obsessions. I dropped in and picked out a bag's worth of chocolates, thinking Autumn might like some. I guessed that she'd be a dark-chocolate kind of girl—strong, and somewhat of an acquired taste.

By the time I got to our "office," she was already there and had prepared an agenda for what we needed to talk about.

I sat down next to her at the table, and we went to work. Twenty minutes later we'd gone through her list.

"What's on your list?" she asked.

I showed her my list. It wasn't as long as hers, of course. We managed to make it through it all in just a few minutes.

"Anything else?" she asked.

"Just this," I said, opening up my bag and showing her what was inside.

She hesitated before politely taking a piece of chocolate from the bag. "Thank you." She pulled a new tissue from a small packet she carried in her purse. "I brushed my teeth before I came here, so I'll wait until later to enjoy it." She placed the chocolate on the tissue and started to fold it up.

"It's dark chocolate with very little sugar."

She stopped wrapping the chocolate. "Oh." She sighed, looking at the chocolate, and licked her lips.

"Also, it's mixed with blueberries, so it's got Vitamin C in it. And crushed almonds. It's actually pretty healthy."

"I see," she said, nodding. "Well, maybe I'll take a tiny taste and have the rest later."

She picked up the chocolate and nibbled at the edge. She savored it for a moment, then said, "Oh my gosh, Nicolas! This is so good!"

"You can call me Nick if you want. I'm glad you like it." I popped an entire piece in my mouth. "Oh, yeah, now we're talking!"

She spent the next thirty seconds wiping her mouth with a tissue. She paused, looked at the partially eaten chocolate for a moment, and then, almost reverently, she placed it in her mouth. She closed her eyes as she let it melt.

I was glad she enjoyed the treat. I opened my textbook, thinking we might want to review our assignment for the next day one last time.

"May I please have another piece?" she asked.

"Well, actually, I was hoping we could just have one piece a day. That way it will last longer."

She frowned. "Look, is it going to kill you to give me one more piece?"

I decided to have a little fun. I grabbed a piece from the bag and stood up. "If you want it, come and get it."

At first she seemed insulted I would involve her in such

a childish game, but then a grin spread across her face, and she stood up and started toward me.

I backed up.

Soon she was chasing me around the room, and we were laughing like kids. She kept trying to grab the chocolate, but she could never reach high enough to get it.

To be completely truthful, I might possibly have mocked her because she couldn't get the chocolate from me. Unfortunately, that made her run back to the table and grab the entire bag.

"That's not fair!" I complained.

"Oh, you poor little boy! Did a mean girl come and take your candy away?"

"Ma'am, I've gonna have to ask you to set the bag on the table and step back," I said in an official cop tone of voice.

"No, never! You can just watch me eat it all!" She popped another piece in her mouth.

What a transformation! Miss Serious had turned into a wild-eyed monster. She laughed, and all I could see was a blob of dark brown where her teeth had once been.

"I'm going to get you for this!" I warned.

She held up her hands and wiggled her fingers. "Bring it!"

With her giggling and me threatening her the way dads do when they pretend to be monsters to their kids, I chased her around the table. To her credit, she was more nimble than I would have predicted.

After a few turns around the table, I jumped up on the table so I could get to her more easily.

It was at that point that the door opened, revealing a very angry, fifty-something librarian. "What are you two doing in here?" she demanded. Her nametag read "M. Keifer, Director, Public Services."

"Uh, studying?" I said, hopping down from the table.

"Don't give me that! I've been watching through the window. You two were frolicking in this conference room!"

Autumn and I traded amused glances.

"Frolicking?" I asked. "What exactly does that mean?"

Never ask a librarian what a word means. She marched to the one-foot-thick dictionary resting on what looked like a heavy wooden music stand and found the definition. "'Frolicking: to play and run about happily.'"

Autumn thought for a moment and then nodded. "Actually, Nick, that might be an accurate description of what we were doing." She was still trying to finish all the chocolate in her mouth.

Mrs. Keifer continued. "Let me remind you that a library is not a place for frolicking. I'm afraid I'm going to have to ask you both to leave this conference room."

"We were studying before you came," Autumn said. "We were just taking a break."

"A frolicking break?" she accused.

"No, a chocolate break," Autumn answered. "Nick brought some chocolate. It's the best I've ever had."

"I doubt that."

"You want to try a piece?" I asked.

"I most certainly do not! What I want is for you both to leave."

"We signed up like we're supposed to," Autumn said.

"Let's see if that's true," she said.

We followed her out to the sign-up sheet.

"Those are our names," Autumn said.

"It doesn't matter. You two have forfeited the opportunity to use this room ever again."

"Why aren't there any people working at these desks?" I asked.

"Budget cuts. And from what I hear, it's only the beginning."

"Oh, I'm sorry," Autumn said. "Look, I know we must have looked like slackers, but we're actually very serious students. I'm a senior with a 4.0 grade point average, and I'm sure Nick is too. Right, Nick?"

"Uh, yeah, almost." I had about a 3.0 grade point average, only one grade point below hers.

"In my sophomore year I received the Hollinger Award," Autumn continued.

It was my turn. "Uh, in third grade I got a penmanship award." It wasn't much, but it was the best I could do.

"You received the Hollinger Award?" Ms. Keifer asked Autumn. "I did too, when I was a student here!"

"So now perhaps you can see that I would ordinarily not be one to frolic in a library," Autumn said. She turned to me. "It was mostly Nick's fault. After giving me one chocolate, he refused to give me another piece, and then he insisted on playing keep-away with the rest of the chocolate. What else could I do?"

Ms. Keifer glared at me; Autumn winked.

"Let's go back inside the conference room and talk this over," Autumn said to Ms. Keifer. "Would you like a piece of chocolate? Nick, you stay out here, okay?"

"You can each have one more piece, but that's all," I whispered to Autumn on her way back into the conference room with Keifer.

22

She gave me an evil smile. "We'll eat as many as we want."

"We'll talk about this later," I said.

"Yes, we will. We will also talk about your egregious behavior."

My mouth dropped open.

She gave me a superior grin. "Look it up. Here's a hint. It starts with the letter *E*." She left me standing there.

Over the next few minutes I watched as the two women made their way through the rest of the chocolate—the entire bag.

When they came out, they seemed friendly enough. Why not? By then they were both on a chocolate high.

"I'll go get your applications and bring them back," Keifer said, and then she left.

"What applications?" I asked Autumn.

"You and I are signing up to be Friends of the Library," she said. "We'll work five hours a week in the library as volunteers."

"You're crazy if you think I'm going to do that."

"In return, we'll have access to the conference room any time we want with our very own key."

"Oh." I paused. "Well, that sounds good."

"We must also supply Ms. Keifer with chocolate."

"What?" I complained.

"It's a small price to pay for the perfect room for us to study in."

"That little bag of chocolate you and Keifer went through today cost me ten dollars."

"You had some too."

"I had one!"

"I'll chip in some money each week to help pay for it," she said.

"You'd better."

We filled out our applications to be Friends of the Library, returned them to Keifer, and then walked outside. We agreed to meet the next day an hour before our class with Penstock.

That night I worried about what I'd do if I didn't get into Harvard Law School. I didn't have an answer to that question.

Also, I might possibly have thought a little about Autumn Jones.

Not much, though. Just a little.

Chapter Three

On Wednesday before class, Autumn and I met in our own private study area. We had only twenty minutes, but that was all we needed. The reading assignment was thirty pages, but most of it was basic introductory material.

We went to class and decided to sit next to each other so we could work together as a team. Godzilla sat on the same row, but a few seats away.

Penstock entered precisely on time.

We were prepared to answer any question based on the reading, but that's not what Penstock wanted.

"I have decided to point out the weaknesses in the arguments presented by those who oppose abortion," he said with a smirk in our direction.

And so he began.

A minute into his tirade, Autumn raised her hand.

He frowned at her. "I will accept no argument based on any religious beliefs or teachings. This is a university class, not some church revival meeting. So what comment do you have to make?"

"Abortion is like killing a baby," she said.

"A fetus doesn't become a baby until it undergoes the birth process."

"I believe the child's spirit enters the body before birth," she argued.

"Spirit? What did I tell you? I will not have you bringing up your religious points of view. I want to center the discussion on rational arguments."

"Rational arguments? Okay, then I assume you would welcome a report of research on young women who have had abortions and who experienced trauma even years later?" She glanced at me as she said it, which was enough for me to Google it. Within ten seconds I had some studies ready for her to read.

He paused. "If you have anything of that nature to say after I've finished, I will give you some time."

"I will look forward to it," Autumn said.

He continued to mock the Right to Life point of view.

"You want to try it?" Autumn whispered to me.

I stood up.

"You don't need to stand up to get my attention, Mr. Baxter. I can see you. What point would you like to make?"

"Just that what you're saying isn't true."

"Are you sure about that? Let's do a case study. Suppose at age sixteen you got a girl pregnant. Her father will not allow her to get an abortion but instead insists you marry the girl. You have to drop out of school and get a job. You work in a dead-end job making minimum wage for the rest of your life. By the time you're forty you realize your whole life has been wasted, but by then it's too late. Is that what you'd want your life to be?"

"No."

"Nobody would. And that's my point. Now suppose you were to help the girl pay for an abortion. She wouldn't have to face the scorn of her friends. She could graduate from high school, go on to college, and embark on a career that will help fulfill whatever dreams she has had. You, too, can go to college and become a . . . What is it you want to become, Mr. Baxter?"

"I want to become a lawyer."

"A lawyer? I should have guessed. Well, Mr. Baxter, if this girl you got pregnant gets an abortion, then you can follow your dream and become a lawyer. Eventually the two of you will marry other people. The two of you will have productive lives, providing for the children you each will have in time. Now are you going to tell me that this girl getting an abortion was a mistake? It is clearly a win-win situation."

"Not for the child who was aborted. All he or she got out of it was an end to whatever life he or she might have had. It's not a win-win situation for that baby."

"It was not a baby. It was a growth, that's all."

"That growth, as you call it, was on its way to becoming a baby."

"And you were once on your way to becoming a rational human being, but that has long since been lost. Sit down. You're wasting my time. And don't say another thing in class today."

He then told the class that Pro-Life supporters were basically uneducated and simply spout whatever garbage their religious leaders give them.

While he was lecturing, Autumn and I continued doing online searches to find additional arguments to bolster our point of view for when Penstock gave her time near the end of class, as he'd promised.

But after forty minutes of nonstop lecturing, it became clear to us that his plan was to run out the clock so there'd be no time left for Autumn.

With only five minutes left in class, Autumn raised her hand. "I'm ready to respond now," she said.

He looked at his watch, flashed us a "gotcha" grin, and announced, "Sorry, no time left. Class dismissed."

"Don't go yet!" she pleaded with the class. "There's still five minutes left."

They didn't care and hurried out. Penstock nodded to us and also left.

Autumn was furious at Penstock. I reached for her hand to try to comfort her, but she shook her head and pulled away.

We returned to the library. She sat on the couch, her shoulders slumped, her head down.

"You okay?" I asked.

"What if someone in our class gets an abortion someday because we couldn't give a valid reason not to?"

A few minutes later she got up and walked out of the room.

I let her go. I didn't know what to say to her to make it better.

The simple fact was that Penstock played hardball, and this time he'd won.

• • •

I wondered if Autumn would drop the class so she wouldn't have to deal with Penstock anymore. If she did, I doubted she'd ever speak to me again.

But Thursday morning at eight she texted me and asked if I could meet her at the library at ten o'clock.

I texted her back: *See you then. I'll bring chocolate.*

By the time I entered the conference room, she was already there. She looked up from her textbook as I sat down across from her.

"Sit next to me, okay?" she asked.

I moved to the other side of the table.

"Will you call on someone to pray?"

I looked around the room. "There's just you and me here," I said.

"I know that."

I cleared my throat. "Autumn, will you say the prayer?" I asked.

She nodded and began to pray. Halfway through, she started to get choked up.

"You okay?" I whispered, opening my eyes to look at her.

She looked at me. "I will be." She closed her eyes and we continued to pray.

After the prayer, she removed her glasses to clean the tears off them.

She looks so much better without glasses, I thought.

"I figured out what we did wrong last time," she said.

"What?"

"The preparations we made were based on the reading assignment. Dr. Penstock doesn't care about the reading assignment. His goal is to sell his point of view."

"Yeah, sure. You're right."

"What we need to do, as quickly as we can, is to prepare arguments for every issue we think he might raise during the semester."

"Okay."

"Let's generate a list of topics. Then we can divide it in two, and each of us will prepare talking points for the ones on our list. This will take a lot of time." She looked up from her notes. "Can I count on you to do your part?"

"Yes."

"Don't say it unless you mean it."

"I mean it."

She nodded. "Thank you. I couldn't do this without you."

"Okay."

"The second thing we failed to do last time was to pray and ask for help."

"That's easy to fix."

"I don't know how you're going to take my next suggestion," she said. "It's really none of my business."

"What is it?"

"Since we will be, in a sense, representing the Church, I'd like to suggest you . . . well . . . wear something other than jeans and a sweatshirt on the days we have class together."

I didn't really appreciate her telling me what to wear, but I had to admit she had a point. I sighed. "Okay, I'll do that."

"Thank you. Okay, just one other thing. I told Ms. Kiefer that if you were available, we'd start our work as Friends of the Library today. Will that work for you?"

"Yeah, I can do that. But if you don't mind, when she's not around, I'm calling her Kiefer."

She nodded. "I'll take a chocolate now, please."

I went to my backpack and took out the bag of chocolates I'd bought on my way to campus.

"How many do you need today?" I asked.

"Just one."

"You sure? You and Kiefer went through the whole bag on Tuesday."

She took a bite of the chocolate and then closed her eyes. "Oh, wow! That's so good! What's in it?"

"Dark chocolate and huckleberries."

An hour later we sought out Kiefer to start our volunteer hours. She took us to a back room where a large table was piled with junk mail. "I need you two to sort through all this back mail. Keep what is relevant or important, and throw the rest away," she said.

"How will we know if it's relevant or important?" Autumn asked.

"If you find anything that describes programs or grants the library can apply for and for which we haven't missed the application deadline, keep them for my review."

"Sounds easy enough," I said.

Five minutes later I was bored. "Let's make a game out of this," I said.

"What kind of a game?"

"We put the trash can in the middle of the floor. We stand here and wad up the papers we're going to throw away, and then we try to lob them into the can. The one who gets the most baskets wins."

"Is that really the most efficient use of our time?"

"Yes, studies have shown that it is," I said with a grin.

"It is not."

"You're afraid of losing, right? You can't take the pressure, can you?"

"I am not afraid."

I took a flyer, crunched it into a ball, and shot. It sailed into the trash can.

"Nothing but net, baby! Nicolas—one, Autumn—zero." I did a little victory dance around her.

She ignored me and kept working. A short time later she walked several flyers over to the trash can and dumped them in.

On her way back to me, I crumpled up a brochure and lobbed it toward the can; it hit her on the shoulder.

She scowled at me. "Do you have to make a game out of everything?"

"Yeah, I do. Look, here's the deal. If I'm not having fun, then I move on to something else. This could be way more enjoyable than it is. I am so bored! When is this going to be over?"

We decided to take a chocolate break. While hers was still in her mouth, she took a flyer, crumpled it into a ball, and tossed it into the trash can.

"Autumn—one, Nicolas—one!" she cried out, doing a victory dance around me. Except mine was better.

After that we had fun and got the work done, too.

• • •

In Friday's class Penstock lectured about how students in his class could get credit for participation. Up until then, nobody except Autumn and me had offered any comments. Who could blame them for staying silent, right?

Penstock explained that at the beginning of each class

he would pick five students at random to either express an opinion or refer to a news story dealing with a current issue. He recommended either *The New York Times* or CNN as reliable sources.

Of course, what happened was totally predictable. The seniors created an e-mail group in which a few students each week would be in charge of finding news or editorial comments that matched Penstock's point of view. They would e-mail the information to everyone else.

It worked out well for everyone. Penstock was happy, the students were happy. When it came time for student participation, everyone was in complete agreement on every issue with Penstock. Except, of course, for Autumn and me.

On that Friday, Penstock asked students picked at random their views about various topics. Strangely enough, they all seemed to agree with him.

On Saturday afternoon, Autumn and I got together in our private office in the library to develop talking points for any topic Dr. Penstock might bring up. Our plan was that, for each topic, one of us would select quotes from the scriptures or from General Authorities, while the other would look for sources that even Penstock would have to recognize as being legitimate.

At seven-thirty, we picked up a pizza and returned with it to our study area.

While we ate, she asked me how old I was.

"Almost twenty-two," I said. In this case *almost* meant that I would turn twenty-two in four months.

"I'm twenty-three."

"So you're older than me?" I said.

"Yes. Older and wiser." She got a mischievous grin on her face. "Is it okay if I call you Preppy?"

"No, it's not."

She laughed. "Then I will."

I thought we'd be going to church together the next day, but she told me she preferred to attend a family ward, even though there was a singles branch meeting in the same building. I had no interest in that, so on Sunday we didn't see each other.

Monday was a holiday, so the library was closed. I called Autumn at noon and asked if she'd like to go to lunch with me. She said she was busy working on another class. I was disappointed but didn't push it.

On Wednesday, at the beginning of Penstock's class, Autumn and I raised our hands. He ignored us, so we stood up.

"What now?" he grumbled.

"Last week, you promised to give us time to present arguments against abortion," Autumn said. "We are prepared to do that now."

"That was last week. You missed your chance. Too bad. Now sit down. Today we are going to talk about war, which I would guess you're both in favor of."

He spent the rest of the class outlining his opposition to war. We gave him a pass on that, since who isn't opposed to war?

On Friday, he must have decided to yank our chain. He began with this statement: "Anyone who believes that God created the Earth is ignorant and uneducated."

This was something I'd spent time preparing for. Autumn looked at me and smiled. "Go get him, Preppy."

I raised my hand.

"Speaking of ignorant and uneducated—Nicolas, do you have a comment?" Penstock asked. The class predictably laughed.

"Yes, I do. May I please have a couple of minutes to make a point?"

"Yes, please do. I'm sure you'll end up making my point for me, but you go ahead and give it your best shot."

I walked quickly to the front of the classroom so I could face the class and began. "First of all, I'd like you to picture ten thousand monkeys sitting at their laptops typing away, pausing only long enough to have a banana and some water once a day. Hour after hour, day after day. The goal of this federally-funded project—your tax dollars at work—is to see how long it will take before one of the monkeys types Abraham Lincoln's Gettysburg Address—without a single error."

"Thank you very much for your elucidating point about monkeys," he said. "Now go take your seat."

"I'm not done yet."

He looked at the clock on the wall. "Out of kindness, I will give you three more minutes."

I looked down at my notes. "The Gettysburg Address contains one thousand and sixty-six characters. My laptop has fifty keys. So let's start at the beginning of Lincoln's Gettysburg Address. A monkey has a one-in-fifty chance of hitting the correct first key, which of course is the letter F. After striking one thousand and sixty-six characters, a monkey's chance of getting the whole thing right is one divided by fifty multiplied by one divided by fifty times . . . well, you get the idea. That number can be visualized by this—"

I uncapped a marker and put a decimal point on the whiteboard. "Now just add one thousand eight hundred and eleven zeros and then write the number one. This is a very small number. In the interest of time, I won't write out all the zeros."

"And your point is?" Dr. Penstock said impatiently.

"If you think monkeys typing randomly to reproduce the Gettysburg Address is unlikely, consider this: The human genome stored on DNA can be compared to instructions stored in a book. That book would be bound in five thousand volumes, and each volume would contain three hundred pages. C'mon, little monkeys, you can do it!" I paused. "Well, actually, maybe not. The universe has not existed long enough to account for this earth and its inhabitants having come together through random chance."

"Forty seconds," Penstock said.

"Sir Francis Crick, co-discoverer of the DNA structure, suggested that space aliens seeded the early earth with genetic material that later evolved to give us the variety we see around us now. If he, a winner of the Nobel Prize, thought *that* was a more reasonable explanation than random chance, then I think we need to at least consider the possibility of intelligent design. And, in fact, many scientists today agree with me that random chance alone is not capable of creating life."

I turned to him and with an impudent grin casually tossed the marker back into its tray. "I rest my case."

"Mr. Baxter, if there are ever any openings for a monkey at the zoo, I suggest you apply," he joked.

The class laughed.

"Let me focus on the questions you've raised—next class period," Penstock said arrogantly.

I sat down next to Autumn. She gave me a big smile. And then she leaned into me and rested her hand on my arm. "Good job!"

"Thanks."

Penstock noticed. "Seeing you two so wrapped up in each other, I'm curious. I assume you two are living together. Is that correct?"

Autumn almost leaped out of her seat. "Dr. Penstock, it is totally inappropriate for you to say that!"

He chuckled. "So you are then, right?"

I stood up. "I can answer that question. No, we are not living together." I glanced down at my laptop. "To help explain why, I will be quoting from a document published by our church. It is entitled 'The Family: A Proclamation to the World': 'We further declare that God has commanded that the sacred powers of procreation are to be employed only between man and woman, lawfully wedded as husband and wife. We declare that the means by which mortal life is created to be divinely appointed. We affirm the sanctity of life and of its importance in God's eternal plan.'"

"Our actions are consistent with that statement," Autumn added.

Penstock smirked. "Well, I'm sure it's just a matter of time. You be sure and report back to class when it happens." He flashed us a lascivious grin. "Who knows, I might even give you both extra credit." The class laughed as he knew they would.

I could tell from his expression, though, that he knew

he'd gone too far. His disdain for us and his need to play to the crowd had taken over his judgment.

"Let's get out of here!" Autumn said to me.

We packed up our books and stormed out of class. In case there might be any uncertainty of our reaction to what he'd said, I made it a point to slam the door on our way out.

We headed straight to the administration building, to the office where sexual harassment charges could be made, and each of us gave a statement about what Penstock had said to us.

An hour later, we each received a call from a department secretary setting up a time when we could meet with Penstock, his department chairman, and the sexual harassment officer for the university. We agreed to meet that afternoon.

At that meeting we each told our story of what had happened in class.

Penstock smiled patronizingly. "I'm sorry you misunderstood what I said."

"Is that the best you can do?" Autumn complained. "That is the lamest apology I've ever heard."

The department chairman told us that he regretted the incident and would in no way try to minimize it. He then spent fifteen minutes minimizing it. His point was that sexual activity among college students was so common that Penstock probably didn't think it was an inappropriate question, and that he was sure no harm was meant.

Autumn explained that she and I came from a background where sexual activity was reserved for marriage and that we were insulted that Dr. Penstock would insinuate in front of the whole class that we were living together, contrary to our beliefs concerning chastity.

"I am sorry for what I said," Penstock finally said. "It will not happen again."

"No, it won't," Autumn said. "You know why? Because there are legal actions a student can take when something like this happens."

"Do you two want to carry this further?" the sexual harassment officer asked us.

"Can Autumn and I go into the hall and discuss this for a minute?" I asked.

The officer agreed.

In the hall, I turned to face her. "We need to get something from this," I said.

"Like what?" she asked.

"How about respect?"

We talked for a few minutes and then returned to the meeting.

I began. "We feel that damage has been done to our reputation among members of the class. We would like the opportunity to present our point of view about subjects discussed in class without Dr. Penstock making derisive comments about us or our church and its teachings."

A flash of anger crossed Dr. Penstock's face, but it only lasted a second. He must have realized we had him.

"My class is one where we explore various positions on issues of importance," Penstock said. "And so, of course, I will continue to welcome students' opinions, as always." He nodded to his department chair, who smiled in approval.

Autumn rolled her eyes and shook her head.

Penstock noticed. "And if these two wish to comment at any time during the class, I will welcome their input."

Everyone turned to us.

"We want a text message the night before about what you plan to discuss the next day in class," I told Penstock.

He grimaced but said, "Fine."

We left.

We were satisfied with this small victory, so to celebrate, we had lunch together.

I asked her about the missionary she was waiting for.

"What do you want to know?" she asked.

"What's his name?" I asked.

"Elder Bonneville."

"Where's he from?"

She started to blush. "Utah, I think."

That seemed strange. "What's his first name?"

"I don't know."

"You're waiting for a guy, and you don't even know his first name or where he's from?" I asked.

"Okay, look, the truth is I'm not actually waiting for him."

"Why did you say you were the first time we went to the library?" I asked.

"I didn't want what we're doing for our class to be about us."

"So tell me about Elder Bonneville," I said.

"For the last six months of my mission, Elder Bonneville and I were in the same district. The first month, he and his companion led the mission in baptisms. The second month my companion and I did. So after that we had fun trying to outdo the other. Also, we attended the same ward and traded off teaching the Gospel Essentials class. Just before I left, he asked if he could write me. I said that would be okay. So we've been writing. That's all there is to it." She sighed. "However, I do respect him a great deal."

"So are you waiting for him or not?"

"No, not really. In a recent letter, though, he asked if he could visit me after his mission, and I said yes. That's the only commitment I've made to him."

"That's a little weird, but, you know, whatever. It doesn't matter. I'm sure after graduation we'll both go our separate ways." That sounded a little harsh, so I added, "Until then, if we can do some good by standing for what we know is right, that will always be a great memory for both of us."

She hesitated a moment, then said, "That's a good way to look at it." Then she added, "I do enjoy working with you."

"Yeah, that's a plus for me too. Also, let me say that if that's what you want, I hope you and Elder Wonderful do get together some day."

"His last name is Bonneville."

I shrugged. "Whatever."

Chapter Four

On Monday, Penstock got even for my typing-monkey analogy.

"Today I am pleased to introduce Dr. Benjamin J. Bashuri from the biology department. He is a noted scholar, winner of the prestigious Presidential Award for excellence in research, and a three-time president of the American Institute of Biological Sciences. Last year he was nominated for the Nobel Prize in Chemistry."

Dr. Bashuri laughed. "Unfortunately, though, I didn't get it."

"Better luck next year, right?" Penstock asked.

"We'll see. By the way, Thomas, if I do happen to win the Nobel Prize this year, the next time you invite me to talk to your class, it's going to cost you much more than a day-old bagel and a lukewarm cup of coffee for my time."

We all laughed at that.

Penstock continued. "I have asked Dr. Bashuri to discuss the scientific reasons intelligent design should not be taught in schools and how we can fight against this intrusion by religious zealots into the realm of science education. Dr. Bashuri, the time is now yours."

I looked at Autumn and sighed. "We're in trouble," I said softly.

"I know."

Dr. Bashuri was charming, persuasive, and thorough. After discussing the theory of evolution and giving examples of it found in recent times, he then suggested that those who championed intelligent design were merely Christians trying to mask their religious fervor with phony science so they could have the Bible taught in schools.

He continued. "This flies in the face of the scientific method and will lead to the teaching of superstitious religious mythology in education as opposed to proven, empirical truths that have been discovered by the great scientists of the last several hundred years." Then he added, "Modern advancements have all been made possible because of scientific and mathematical expertise. Replace those with creationist blather, and I fear for our future."

Bashuri then began a PowerPoint presentation, which, of course, was simply an invitation for the class to take a nap.

He droned on and on. To tell you the truth, I had no idea what he was talking about.

Autumn leaned over to me and whispered. "So, Preppy, what's your plan?"

"Me? Why can't you do something?"

"You're the one who studied intelligent design."

"We're not in this guy's league. I mean, he could get a Nobel Prize this year. What do you want me to do? Sing a Primary song to him?"

"Penstock brought him here because he thinks we'll be too intimidated to stand up to him. Think of a probing question you can ask him."

"Yeah, right," I scoffed.

"Just say something, okay?"

Bashuri finished his presentation, and Penstock turned on the lights.

I raised my hand.

Penstock was eagerly waiting. "We have a question, Dr. Bashuri, from the young man I was telling you about before class."

"What is your question?" Dr. Bashuri asked.

I stood up. "Okay, suppose you have a bunch of monkeys and you want them to type the Gettysburg Address . . ."

Dr. Bashuri and Dr. Penstock looked at each other as though they couldn't believe what they were hearing and then began laughing—so hard they couldn't stop.

The class joined in too. My voice faded out. I felt like a complete idiot.

When the laughter finally died down, I cleared my throat and continued. "It would take a long time, right? Well, it would take even longer to explain the world we live in if you just assumed random events."

Dr. Bashuri asked, "Are you familiar with the recent paper by Billingsley and Huang presented at the American Association for the Advancement of Science meeting held in Washington D.C. a couple of months ago?"

I sighed. "Uh . . . no."

"Well, certainly you've read the recent groundbreaking paper by Edelman and Chambers, right?"

"Not really."

His eyebrows shot up. "You haven't? Well then, I suggest you read those papers first, and then perhaps we can have an intelligent discussion about intelligent design." He flashed me a big smile.

Penstock nodded. "Perhaps we could have an even more coherent discussion if you send one of those typing monkeys in your place."

More laughter. Everyone was in such a good mood at my expense.

Penstock turned to the rest of the class. "Are there any serious questions for Dr. Bashuri?"

Nobody had any questions, and class was dismissed.

I was the first one out of the classroom. I didn't want to talk to Autumn. I was angry at her for baiting me into asking Bashuri a question.

She caught up with me and walked beside me. I wouldn't even look at her.

"Can I buy you some hot chocolate?" she asked.

"No!" I snapped, walking even faster.

"We need to talk."

I stopped to confront her. "You know what? I am so tired of talking to you! It only gets me into trouble."

"If you think you're in trouble just for asking a question in class, then you're definitely not the man I thought you were."

That made me even more mad. I let her have it. "I have never been the man you thought I was because, let's face it, I'm not in Elder Wonderful's class. So let's just quit seeing each other, and then we'll both be happier."

I tried to walk away, but she kept up with me. "We can't quit now," she said.

45

"Oh, really? Why's that?"

"Because for some people in the class we'll be the only members of the Church they will ever come in contact with. We might lose the battle of Penstock, but we can't just quit."

"I hate being laughed at!"

"I know. Everyone does."

"You know what? I'm going back to my place to study."

"We're scheduled to do our volunteer work at the library."

Without even turning around to face her, I threw up my hands as I walked away. "Find some other clown, okay?"

I had gone about ten steps when she called out. "Nick!"

I turned to face her. "What?"

She had tears in her eyes. "Please don't walk away from this. I can't do this without you. I need your help."

"Why do you need me? I'm a complete washout! You know it! I know it! Penstock knows it! The entire class knows it!"

"Washout? Where do you get that? That's not what you are."

"Look, let's face the truth. I'm just an ordinary guy. There's nothing special about me."

"I don't agree. I think you're awesome. Please don't leave me to face Penstock alone. Please stay with me."

I stood there for a minute, staring at the ground, fighting the anger and embarrassment I was feeling. How could I say no to her? I shook my head and walked back to her.

We went to the library and talked. It was good. I'm no Elder Wonderful, you understand. But, even so, I felt good that she felt like she needed me, that she let me in on her thoughts, that she asked my advice, that she looked on the bright side even when I bombed out. She assured me that Father in Heaven would help us because we were embarked on a noble cause.

I knew that I'd miss her if I walked away. Why? Because when I was with her, I wanted to be better. I wanted to be noble. I wanted to be kind. I wanted to be brave. I wanted to slay her every dragon and fight her every adversary.

That's why I stayed. Not because of any hope of us having any kind of a future together.

Chapter Five

With Penstock under the administration's magnifying glass because of our complaints against him, he stopped spewing out radical ideologies, but, instead, let the students do it for him. He began to spend half the class time having students report on what they'd seen on TV or read about current events. Those who supported his position on a given issue received a warm response and an A for their efforts. Autumn and I, on the other hand, received a scowl and a C+.

By this time, I had painfully realized that I probably wasn't going to get an A in the class and that Harvard Law School might not be in my future after all.

The only thing that kept me going was that, against my better judgment, I was falling in love with Autumn. It's not something I ever brought up though. I knew my role, and I played it well.

On a dreary Tuesday the first week in February, we took a walk together between classes. It was a beautiful winter day, cold but sunny. We walked through a large park across from campus.

I needed a break from being responsible. "What would you think if I chased you through the park right now?" I asked.

"You want to chase me through the park?" she asked.

"Yes, I do."

"Why?"

"I want to hear you giggle the way you did when we were playing keep-away with the chocolate."

"Why do you want me to giggle?"

"Don't you ever get tired of being a grown-up? Why do we always have to deal with each other as responsible adults? Just once I want to be the boy who chased you at recess and made you laugh."

"I see." She stood there looking curiously at me. "I'm not sure what to say. Actually, I don't ever remember a boy chasing me at recess."

If she had immediately agreed to my suggestion, it would have been okay. But now that she insisted on analyzing it, it left me feeling foolish. "Just forget it, okay? I'm sure you have better things to do."

She was still confused. "No, no, I just need to understand where this is coming from, that's all."

I wanted to drop the subject, but I blundered on. "I was just hoping we could recreate the kind of spontaneous joy kids have when they're having fun," I explained.

"I see. So, in a way, this is like an experiment, right?"

"Yeah, I guess so."

"Okay, well, let's try it and see how it goes. I'm going to start running away from you now." And she did.

That wasn't how it was supposed to work. This wasn't something I wanted to talk about. I just wanted to do it.

I stood there, watching her run halfheartedly through the snow, weaving her way between the trees. When I finally started after her, it felt amazingly awkward. I knew she was only doing it for me. She wasn't laughing. She wasn't giggling. Actually, she wasn't even *running*—just a slow jog. Knowing her, I figured she was probably timing herself.

"I am coming to get you," I called out tepidly.

"Okay, commence the chasing," she called back. Yes, she actually said that.

She ran a lot faster than I thought she could, and I stopped to take off my coat so I wouldn't get too sweaty.

When we came to the edge of the park, she stopped. "Is that what you were hoping for?" she asked.

"Yeah, that was real good," I said glumly.

On the other side of the street was the university with all its boring adult responsibilities. I was ready to give up and go back to the library. *It's over,* I thought. *This was such a disaster.*

I walked toward her slowly, disappointed she couldn't give me what I needed. Which really wasn't much. I just wanted to have fun.

"Thanks," I said with little enthusiasm.

She looked into my eyes for a long time, nodded her head slowly, and then she suddenly grabbed my coat and ran back into the park.

"Hey, come back!" I yelled.

"If you want this, Preppy, come get it!" she called out, waving my coat in the air.

And so I ran after her.

This was better. I even did my evil villain imitation. "Resistance is futile! You must stop now!"

There she was—the girl with a 4.0 grade point average, a Hollinger Award recipient, and a returned missionary—running through a park giggling and daring me to catch her if I could. And there I was, lumbering after her and roaring like a bear.

She stopped and waited for me to catch up. "Can't you run any faster than that?" she asked.

"I'm holding back."

"Why?"

"Because I like chasing you."

"You'd like it more if you actually caught me," she teased.

"Why's that?"

She chuckled. "Catch me and you'll find out."

I approached her slowly, waiting for her to bolt away from me.

But this time she didn't. We stood facing each other. So I kissed her.

She relaxed in my arms and didn't pull away. Not even after like twenty seconds. Not even when some motorists honked as they passed us.

When we separated, she had a big smile on her face. "You were right. That was fun, wasn't it?" she said.

"Yeah, it was!"

Almost immediately, though, I could see the embarrassment start to creep into her mind. "So, uh, help me out here. Do you really think this is something we should be doing?" she asked.

"Are you talking about the chasing or the kissing?

Because given a choice, I'm going to go for the kissing every time."

She thought about it and then nodded. "Okay, I guess I agree, although we don't need to give up the chasing, either."

I couldn't believe what she was saying. "Are you serious?"

She nodded. "Of course, the kissing would have to be . . . you know, within certain bounds and, well, appropriate."

"Totally. I'm all for appropriate."

"So we're okay with this?" she asked.

Her cheeks were red from all the running, and she was smiling. At that moment I thought she was the most beautiful girl I'd ever known.

"Yes, I believe we are," I said in answer to her question.

She glanced at her watch. "We'd probably better get back."

I nodded. "Yeah, maybe."

She handed me my coat. I put it on, then held her hand as we headed toward the library.

"Let's agree to something though," I said.

"What?"

"I don't want to talk about where this is headed. I just want it to be what it is . . . with no editorial comments. If we overanalyze it, I'm afraid it will crumble like a house of cards."

She nodded. "You're probably right."

We stopped just before going back into the library. She turned to face me. "Okay. I let you chase me through the park. Will you do something for me?"

"What?"

"Come home with me this weekend. I want you to meet my mom and dad."

I panicked. "What? Why? I thought—"

"Relax. It's not because we're getting serious and I want to see if they approve of you. We both have plans after graduation. You're going to Harvard fall semester, and I'm planning on getting a good job so I can pay off my student loans. So we're probably not going to be getting together . . . you know, like permanently . . ."

"I believe the term is *marriage*," I said.

She nodded. "Right. Look, I'm okay with our agreement that all this is just temporary."

"Good," I said. "So why do you want me to come home with you?"

"I want you to meet my dad. He's taught me a lot. I want him to teach you what he's learned from life."

I realized she was probably just trying to help me. "Okay, I'll come with you."

"Thank you. I'll call and tell them we're coming." She paused. "And why."

We left on Friday after Penstock's class. She drove her car because mine was basically a junker in desperate need of repairs.

The closer we got to her house, the more nervous we both became. I'd never gone home with a girl to meet her folks. I was afraid I'd mess up, and they'd tell Autumn she was wasting her time with me. Which she probably already knew.

As she drove, she told me about the town where she had grown up and recalled some experiences from those years. She had always been a good student, and it sounded like she had a lot of friends. When we were finally on the street where her parents' home was located, she pointed out the house where her best friend had lived and a big tree she had fallen out of and broken her arm when she was in the fourth grade. It was fun for me to see how enthusiastic she was about going home.

We pulled into her driveway, and she said we could get our things from the trunk later. She grabbed my hand as we ran up the porch stairs and into the house.

"We're here!" she called out.

Her mom and dad hurried into the front hallway to greet us.

I was surprised to see her dad. I didn't know what I had expected, but he was a very large man. Except for a line of hair along the sides of his head, he was completely bald. He looked as though he might have been athletic once, but he now had a pretty big belly. His natural speaking voice was raspy, as though he were a smoker, which wasn't the case. Even in normal conversation, he had the voice of a football coach yelling to his players on the field. I suddenly realized why it was that when Autumn spoke up in Penstock's class, everyone could hear her. She'd inherited it from her dad.

When I reached out to shake his hand, he pulled me close and gave me a rib-crushing hug. "Welcome home, son."

Autumn was embarrassed. "Dad, he's not your son."

"He's somebody's son, though, right?"

She sighed. "I suppose."

Autumn's mom was an older version of her daughter. They had the same color hair and eyes, and her mother had retained her slim body. Mrs. Jones also hugged me, but not so enthusiastically as her husband.

We returned to the car to get our things. "Your dad must not have gotten the memo, right?" I asked Autumn.

She smiled. "My dad never gets the memo. He dances to his own tune. Always has, always will."

Autumn's mom stood on the porch to hold the door open for us. "Nick, we are so happy to finally meet you. Autumn has told us so many wonderful things about you."

"It's great to meet you both as well." I'd purposely chosen to say *as well* to impress her folks. I think it sounds much more impressive than if I'd said, "It's great to meet you too." It's those little things that add up over time, right?

We had roasted chicken for dinner. When the platter of chicken came to me, instead of choosing a leg like I normally would, I chose a slice of white meat. I didn't want Autumn's parents to see me picking up the drumstick like I was some kind of caveman. Also, I didn't put gravy on my potatoes. Less chance of spilling some on my shirt.

Education was a big deal in Autumn's family, and her brother and sister were both away at school—her sister at BYU and her brother at Purdue.

"Autumn says you hope to be going to Harvard Law School in the fall," her dad boomed.

"That's right. I hope to."

"Why do you want to be a lawyer?" he asked.

"My dad has a law firm, and he wants me to come work for him—maybe even be a partner some day."

"What kind of law does your father do?" he asked.

"Mostly contracts, wills, and estate management."

He was trying not to sound negative, and it almost worked. "Sounds boring to me, but, hey, if that's what you want to do, go for it, son."

Once again Autumn cringed at her dad calling me "son."

The dinner conversation turned to what Autumn and I were trying to do in Penstock's class. While she talked, I hunkered down and put all my attention into chewing my food very slowly so no one would ask me any questions.

The first thing her dad insisted on after we'd eaten was to have me watch a DVD they'd made out of all the home movies they'd taken as Autumn was growing up.

She and her sister were amazingly cute as little girls. And judging by the number of times her brother was shown swimming, I wasn't at all surprised to learn he was a water polo player. In many of the shots, Autumn was involved in some childlike fun—learning to ride her two-wheeled bike, climbing on some monkey bars, or running through the sprinklers in her swimming suit. For some reason that enchanted me, maybe because I wanted her to be as open to having fun now as she had been then.

Autumn, for her part, blushed through most of it.

"So what do you think? Would you like to have a daughter like that some day?" her dad asked me.

"I would, actually."

"Well, there's only one way to capture at least half of the same genes she has. You know what I'm talking about, right?"

Autumn groaned. "Dad, please don't do this."

Her dad continued. "And that's to marry this beautiful girl."

"I am so sorry," Autumn leaned over and whispered to me.

"Who's ready for dessert?" her mom asked as a diversionary tactic.

"I am!" Autumn cried out. "I'll help you dish it up!" she said, bolting for the kitchen.

As soon as Autumn got to the kitchen, she must have realized her dad and I were alone—and who knew what else he'd say to me. She rushed back and asked if I could help too. I was more than happy to escape whatever else her dad might say about me marrying his daughter.

After dessert, Autumn asked me to come with her on a ride to see the town. "Truth is, I've got to get out of here," she confided in me.

So we left. She asked me to drive her car.

At my insistence she showed me her grade school, her junior high, and finally her high school. "Can you stop here for a minute?" she asked as we entered the high school parking lot.

"Sure."

There were still maybe seventy cars in the parking lot, and people were going in and out. We could hear the sounds of a basketball game going on in the gym.

"First of all, I need to apologize for my dad," she said, staring straight ahead at the school.

"It's okay. Don't worry about it."

"He's a mayor, so he's used to getting his own way."

"Look, it's okay. If I'd taken you home with me, my mom would probably have been even worse. The way I look at it, spoiling grandkids is the only thing our folks have to look forward to."

She let out a big sigh and rested her head back on the seat. "Thank you for being so understanding."

"No problem. So this was your high school?"

"Uh-huh."

"Did you have fun here?"

"Oh, yeah! It was great. I loved high school."

"Really? A lot of people I know hated it."

She looked over at me. "Did you?"

"It was okay, but I don't know that I'd ever want to go back. I was glad to move on."

She smiled. "My friends and I had a great time. I loved school, and I loved all the activities. Hey, you want me to give you the tour?"

"If you want, sure."

We walked through the mostly empty halls. She pointed out where she'd had various classes and told me about the teachers who'd helped her the most.

We ended up in the gym, which was filled with people watching the game.

"I was chairman of the prom committee my junior and senior year," she said. "It took a lot of time planning and decorating and taking everything down afterward. And, of course, keeping the punch bowl full."

"I'm curious. How did you estimate how many refreshments you'd need for something like that?"

"Well, first of all, most of the students had bought tickets by the Wednesday before. So you just had to estimate how many more might be deciding at the last minute."

"Okay."

"But then it gets more complicated."

"How's that?"

"Well, you have parents coming and watching their kids from the top of the bleachers, so, you know, it's a good thing to have some punch for them, too."

"Okay, so what do you do? Just guess?"

"I would make an estimate and then add ten percent because you have to have extra in case someone spikes the punch bowl. If that happens, you have to throw it all out and make more."

"So you had this all figured out?"

"Yeah, pretty much. It worked out okay."

"So you were amazing even in high school. I wish I'd known you then. Did you have a date for the prom your junior or senior year?"

"No. I was the only LDS girl in school. And everyone knew I didn't drink or use drugs or sleep around. So, no prom dates for me. But it was okay. There wasn't anyone I wanted to go with anyway."

"Oh."

"Did you go to your proms?" she asked.

"Yeah, I did."

"How was it?"

"My junior year was okay. The girl didn't drink, so that was good. It was the only good thing, actually."

"What wasn't good about it?"

"She gave me pamphlets her minister had given her. The pamphlet said that Mormons aren't Christian, and throughout the night, she kept talking to me about it. We didn't really hit it off."

"What about your senior year?" she asked.

"In our first ten minutes together, my date confided in me that she was pregnant by another guy."

"What did you do?"

"We talked about the possible choices she could make." I sighed. "I tried to help her see that getting an abortion would not be the best choice for her. I offered to have someone from LDS Family Services talk to her."

"What did she do?"

"She ended up getting an abortion. After that, she ducked whenever she saw me coming down the hall."

"Oh."

A few minutes later we returned to the car. When I made my move and put my arm around her, she started laughing.

"What?" I asked.

"You're not actually thinking about kissing me in a high school parking lot, are you?"

"What would be wrong with that?" I asked.

"What are you trying to do, make all your unfulfilled high school fantasies come true?"

"Maybe."

"C'mon, Nick, we're seniors in college. If you want to kiss me, I suggest you find some place with a little more gravitas than a high school parking lot, okay?"

"Gravitas?"

She shook her head. "I knew I should have brought a dictionary for you."

I acted insulted. "I know what *gravitas* means."

"What does it mean?"

"Well, it's like gravity, only . . . uh . . . heavier." I loved to make her laugh, and she didn't disappoint me.

"I am so hoping this is your sense of humor in action and not your true intellect manifesting itself," she said.

"Give me a break, okay? My question for you is—where can I find a place in this town with enough gravitas so you'll let me kiss you?"

She shrugged. "I have no idea. To tell you the truth, I haven't spent a lot of time thinking about this."

So for the next half hour I drove around town, hunting for a grown-up place to kiss. I tried the mall parking lot, the church parking lot, the post office parking lot. Each time, when I pulled in and parked, turning toward her like I was about to kiss her, she'd start laughing. "Not here!"

Finally I pulled into a mortuary parking lot. "There's no place with more gravitas than this! So, whataya say, cupcake, let's get at it, okay?"

That totally broke her up. I felt good about that, although I realized it probably wasn't helping my chances to actually kiss her.

Mimicking a line from *The Princess Bride,* I called out, "Death is what bwings us to-gev-uh today."

She laughed but not as much. "Please stop," she pleaded. "My sides are hurting so much."

I nodded and drove back to her house. I didn't think she'd want her parents seeing us kiss, so I got out of the car and walked around and opened her door.

On her porch she stopped and looked at me a certain way, and so I held her in my arms and kissed her.

"This is good," she said softly.

"Gravitas-wise, you mean?"

"Yeah, pretty much."

I kissed her again. "I know we promised each other we wouldn't talk about this, but do you think we should?" I asked.

"Talk about what?"

"This." I kissed her again. "What we're doing, and why we're doing it."

"Do you want to?" she asked.

I sighed. "I don't know."

"We can talk about it if you want to. We talk about everything else."

I sighed. "The problem is, if we talk about it, then that might be the end of it. And the problem with that is, well, I like this very much."

"Me too." She sighed. "My biggest problem is that I'm not sure what context to put it in."

I nodded, perhaps a little too much. "I know. That's totally it! It's all about context, right?"

She smiled. "Do you know what the word *context* means?"

"If I say no, will you still let me kiss you?"

"I'm not sure," she teased.

"Then let me assure you that I know what it means."

"Tell me what it means," she asked.

Somehow that broke the seriousness. "It's like a contest except . . . it has . . . more gravitas."

She laughed and then kissed me on the cheek. "You want to know something? I've never had so much fun in my life with a guy than I have every day we're together. You're the best friend I've ever had."

The good news was she enjoyed being with me. The bad news was that she used the word *friend.* That couldn't be good.

She sighed. "Actually, maybe we should talk . . . you know . . . about us."

"Okay, but not now. Not this weekend. Not while I'm here at your folks' place. I'm under enough pressure just being here."

"Okay, some other time then. Let's go inside," she said.

"One more kiss . . . please . . . to put things in context," I said.

"You know what? I'm all about context."

And so we kissed one more time and then headed into her house.

"Just so we're in agreement, that was our last kiss for the night, okay?" she said once we got inside.

"Okay."

Her folks had already gone to bed. In the kitchen we rummaged through the refrigerator, pulling out things to eat.

"Will you watch a movie with me?" she asked.

"What movie?"

She shook her head. "You're going to think it's dumb."

"No, I won't."

"I'm a little embarrassed to say this, but when I was a kid, I loved to watch *Scooby-Doo*. I think I saw every episode they made. More than anything, I wanted to be Velma. She's the smart one who wears glasses. Did you ever watch it?"

"No, not really, but you know, I'm willing to give it a try. Are we going to watch every episode? That might take a while."

"No, we're going watch the prequel movie that came out recently. It's called *Scooby-Doo! The Mystery Begins*. It will get you up to speed."

I shrugged. "Okay, let's do it."

I kept dozing off during the movie. I felt guilty about falling asleep, so I tried to stay awake by eating chips and salsa.

"Okay, pay attention now!" she said. "This is the whole reason we're watching."

The movie was almost over, and the Scooby-Doo team

had just solved their first crime. The characters were about to go their separate ways, but as they started to walk away, they suddenly learned about another mystery that needed to be solved. Velma told them all about "strange goings-on in the museum," and that was enough to keep them together as a team.

I leaned back on the couch, and Autumn scooted closer to me. "All my life I've wanted someone to work together with, like Velma. Right now you're the closest thing I've got because of what we're trying to do in Penstock's class. Every time we plan what we're going to say in class, I think to myself as we're going to class, *Here we go again, off for another adventure!*"

"Which one of the guys am I?"

"You choose."

"Not the nerdy guy. The other one."

"That's Fred. You'd be a good Fred."

We returned to the kitchen. "You okay with cereal for a snack?" she asked.

"That'd be great."

They had an entire shelf filled with cereal boxes. I went with Honey Nut Cheerios while she predictably chose Kashi.

"I'm grateful to you for coming here with me," she said as we ate.

"I'm enjoying getting to know you better," I said.

"I trust you more than any other guy I've ever known."

"Trust is good."

"Yeah, it is."

We talked for another hour.

"We need to get some sleep," she finally said.

"Yeah, probably."

She hesitated. "What would you think about us having family prayer?" she asked.

I paused. "I don't know. We could, I guess, except for the fact we're not family."

"No, we're not. What would be the problem?"

I cleared my throat. "Well, to tell you the truth, it might be a little too . . . well . . . *intimate* for two people who happen to have one class together."

"Oh."

I didn't feel like I was making much sense. "I didn't mean intimate in the usual sense of the word."

"I know."

"The thing is, after the semester is over, we're both going our separate ways," I said.

"That's true. Okay, we don't need to have family prayer."

I nodded. "I think that would be for the best." I paused. "To tell you the truth, after we split, I'm afraid I'm going to spend time thinking about this weekend, wishing I could live it over and over."

"I totally agree. All right then, good night."

She went to her room and closed the door.

After using the bathroom I went into her brother's room and got into bed. Even though I was tired, I couldn't go to sleep. I kept beating myself up for refusing to have family prayer with her. After a half hour or so, I finally fell asleep.

Chapter Six

At eight-thirty the next morning, Autumn knocked on my bedroom door.

"Nick, are you up yet?"

I sat up in bed. Still groggy, I called out, "Yes, I am."

"Are you decent?"

Because I had just woken up, the question stumped me. "Uh, in what sense?"

She laughed. "Can I come in?"

"I guess."

She opened the door. "You're still in bed?"

I looked around at my surroundings. "Yeah, I guess I am."

"Why did you tell me to come in then?"

"I don't know."

"Hurry, get dressed—my dad wants to take us to his office and show us around."

"I need to shave first."

She started laughing. "What for? You could go a week without shaving. Come on, let's go."

"Shut the door on your way out."

She scowled at me. "Like I wouldn't have thought of that myself, right?"

I quickly showered, shaved, and dressed. When I finally entered the kitchen, she had a plate of food prepared for me: eggs, bacon, pancakes, and orange juice.

"Did you make any of this?" I asked.

"Yes, I did."

"Which part?"

She hesitated. "The orange juice."

"What did you do?"

"It was frozen and I mixed it."

"So what you're saying is your mom cooked most of this, right?"

"No, my dad made breakfast. And I happen to think that's a good tradition."

"I'm sure you do." I sat down to eat.

"We already blessed it," she said. "So just go ahead."

I had only eaten four bites when her dad came in. "So are you two ready?"

I slid the fried egg onto a pancake and folded it up. "I'm ready."

"Finish your orange juice," Autumn instructed me. "I went to a lot of trouble to make it for you."

I chugged it down. "I bet you even stirred it, didn't you? How many times?"

"Three or four."

"What a woman!"

She pretended to be mad, but her grin gave her away. "Respect the orange juice, Preppy!"

I stuck out my tongue at her.

"Are you always this way when you first get up?" she asked.

"I was thinking the same thing about you," I said.

On our drive to her dad's office, I sat in the front seat with her dad and Autumn sat in the backseat. As he drove us around town, he pointed out improvements the city had made while he'd been mayor.

Because it was a Saturday, the city office building was empty. We ended up in a conference room with a long table, three chairs on each side, and one chair at the head of the table. On the wall was a whiteboard.

Her dad was in charge. "Every morning at seven o'clock, we have a one-hour staff meeting. I've got the chief of police, the director of the sewage treatment center, the guy who runs our garbage collection system, a street repair foreman, and a lawyer we have on retainer. We discuss everything that needs to be done that day. Assignments are made at every meeting. So the first thing we do when we get together is get a progress report about previous assignments, and then we move on to new business. Every complaint is logged in and discussed. Someone is assigned to make a personal phone call to each person who called with a complaint, and we outline whatever course of action we decide on. Nobody is left hanging with a complaint for more than twenty-four hours. Of course, some days we can't completely solve the problem because of a lack of resources, but we do what we can."

While he talked, Autumn quietly pulled her backpack onto her lap, under the table and out of her dad's sight. She reached into it and pulled out a small bag of chocolates from our favorite shop.

She palmed a piece of chocolate and slid it over to me.

I took it, and when her dad had turned his back to us to write on the whiteboard, I popped it in my mouth.

"Bless you, my child," I whispered in her ear.

"I knew you'd need it. My dad sometimes doesn't know when to stop talking," she confided.

"I love dark chocolate," I whispered.

"I know. Me too."

At the next opportune moment, she put a piece of chocolate in her mouth. When her dad turned around to face us, we were both extremely happy.

Next he took us on a tour of all the city offices. To tell you the truth, if it hadn't been for Autumn sneaking chocolate to me every few minutes, I'd have never made it.

Twenty minutes later, he escorted us back to the conference room.

"Now, let's see what I can do for you two. Tell me about this class you're taking, and what you've done so far."

We brought him up to speed.

Autumn had me tell about my analogy about the typing monkeys that I'd given in class one day and then about Penstock's guest lecturer Dr. Bashuri the next class period—and how badly those had gone.

"What questions did Dr. Bashuri ask you?"

"He asked me if I'd read two scientific papers. I hadn't even heard of either one of them."

"Do you think he really expected you to have read those papers?" her dad asked me.

"No."

"Then why did he ask?"

"To make me look like I didn't know what I was talking about," I said.

"Did he actually refute your argument?"

"No. He did spend a lot of time lecturing on the scientific proof of evolution though."

"Like what?"

"Birds and butterflies and things like that," I said.

"Are you talking about a bird turning into a butterfly?"

"No, not really. Uh, I didn't follow all of it, but it was like birds' beaks changing so they can crack open nuts better."

"Of course birds can change in order to adapt to a changing environment. But that's not what people usually mean when they talk about evolution, is it?"

"No. They believe that all life developed due to random processes."

He got up and paced back and forth. I looked at Autumn who shrugged her shoulders. "He does that when he's thinking."

I noticed she had taken off her shoes, so she only had on socks. I removed my right shoe and slid my foot on top of hers.

She looked at me, got a big smile on her face, and slid her foot away. So naturally my foot chased her foot.

Her dad went to the whiteboard, picked up a marker, and turned to us.

We looked serious and interested.

"Let me ask you both a question," her dad said. "What would you say is your primary objective in this class?"

Her foot was resting on top of mine. She put her hand

over her mouth to hide her smile. Then she suddenly slammed her heel down on my toes.

It didn't hurt, but I wanted her to think it had. "Ugh!" I groaned.

"Nick, I'm interested in what you're thinking right now," her dad said.

"I am too," Autumn said with an innocent look on her face. "Please tell us what you're feeling," she said.

"I will get you for this," I whispered.

I faced her dad at the whiteboard. "Well, the thing is, Dr. Penstock does nothing but spew out radical ideas."

"So your goal is to . . . ?" her dad asked.

"To slow him down. To present another point of view," I said.

"Why? Do you think you can convince him that you're right?"

Autumn slid her feet away from mine so she could be serious. "No, that isn't our goal," she said. "We'll never convince him of anything."

"If you know Dr. Penstock is not going to change his mind about the issues he brings up, what do you want to accomplish?" her dad asked.

Autumn bent down and put her shoes back on, and I slipped my foot back into my shoe.

"What do you think, Preppy?" she asked.

"It's for the other students in the class," I said to her.

She nodded.

"I can't hear you two when you're mumbling," her dad said.

"We're doing this for the others in the class," she said loud enough for her dad to hear.

"So that they will what?"

"So that . . . they won't be brainwashed," I said.

"Why do you care if they accept political views that you don't necessarily favor? I mean, why is that important to you? Is it worth risking your grades? Your future? The people in your class are basically good people, right? So what if they don't believe everything you do?"

We didn't have an immediate answer. He tossed the marker on the whiteboard tray and walked out. "I need to run an errand. I'll be back in ten minutes."

He started to leave, but just before he reached the door, he turned to us.

"Oh, by the way, don't think I didn't see you two playing footsie under the table."

And then he left.

"We're so busted," I said with an embarrassed grin.

"Yeah, not much escapes my dad. Of course in high school there wasn't much for him to catch me at."

"So what are we going to tell your dad about Penstock when he comes back?" I asked.

"Let's use the whiteboard and put up some possibilities." Autumn handed me a colored marker. "Okay, you do the writing."

"Well, first of all, we're never going to win a debate with Penstock," I said, writing it on the board.

"I agree. It's not just him we have to contend with. It's all his faculty buddies that he can invite in to tear our arguments apart."

I wrote down "He's got smart friends" on the board. Then I said, "It's not too likely we're going to change the opinion of anybody in the class, either."

"Why do you say that?" Autumn asked.

"Because most of them don't care. They just want to get a good grade. Also, Penstock is an authority figure, so they naturally respect him."

"So why *are* we doing this?" she asked. "I mean, a year from now, what difference will any of this make?"

"It might not make any difference, except we'll know we stood up for what we believed in," I said, and wrote: "We need to stand up for our beliefs."

"I guess that's worth something," she said.

I picked up the eraser from the whiteboard tray, turned, and tossed it into a trash basket. "Preppy—one, Autumn—zero."

She shook her head but grinned at me anyway. "You're such a *guy*!"

I retrieved the eraser and handed it to her. She shot and missed.

"Oh, that's a real heartbreak there," I said, pretending to be sympathetic. "My turn now." I tried it again and missed.

She made it on her second shot. "Whoa, look what we have here! A tie game!" she said, pumping her fist.

By the time her dad returned, we'd moved on to having a contest to see how far we could slide in our stocking feet by running from her dad's office into the hall. It was a Saturday, and there was no one in the building to see us.

Through one of the big windows, we saw him pull into his parking stall outside the city office. We hurried back to the whiteboard and pretended to be in a serious discussion.

"Well, what have you come up with?" he asked as he came in.

"This," I said, pointing to what we'd written on the whiteboard.

He read our notes and nodded. "Good, you're on the right track. The reason I went home was to get a book. It's called *Memorable Stories and Parables* by Boyd K. Packer. Let me summarize part of it, and then I'll read something to you. President Packer was about to finish up his doctorate degree and was in a class with just three other students. One of the other students took issue with President Packer, and they continued to debate over several class periods. Their instructor moderated the discussion."

Then he began reading President Packer's words: "'So there we were, two contestants. . . . The issue grew more important, and each day I left the class feeling a greater failure. Why should this concern me? It concerned me because I was *right* and he was wrong, and I knew it and I thought he knew it, and yet he was able to best me in every discussion. Each day I felt more inadequate, more foolish, and more tempted to capitulate.'"

"We can relate with that," Autumn said.

Her dad continued, "Then one of the most important experiences of his entire education occurred. One of the other students in the class said to President Packer: 'You're losing, aren't you?'

"President Packer then said, 'There was no pride left to prevent me from consenting to the obvious. "Yes, I'm losing."'

"The other student quickly told President Packer how he viewed the situation. 'The trouble with you,' he said, 'is that you are fighting out of context.'

"President Packer wasn't sure what that meant, and his fellow student didn't explain."

Autumn leaned over to me and asked quietly. "Do you need to look up the definition of the word *context*?"

"No, I'm good," I said.

Autumn's dad continued to read: "'It wasn't the grade or the credit I was concerned about—it was bigger than that. I was being beaten and humiliated in my efforts to defend a principle that was true. The statement, "You are fighting out of context" stayed in my mind. Finally, in my humiliation, I went before the Lord in prayer. Then I knew.

"'The next day we returned to class, this time to stay in context. When the debate was renewed, instead of mumbling some stilted, sophisticated, philosophical statement, calculated to show I was conversant with philosophical terminology and had read a book or two . . . I stayed in context.

"'Suddenly the tables were turned. I was rescued from defeat, and I learned a lesson I would not forget.'

"President Packer concluded with this advice:

"'Certainly you will not be able to persuade everyone to accept your views. Be wise enough to know when not to try. You can, however, inform people clearly enough that, accept them or not, they know what your convictions are. In this way teach faith, repentance, baptism. . . . '"

Autumn's dad read quietly to himself, turned the page, continued reading, nodded, and said, "Okay, listen to this:

"'The bottom line is that we must never allow ourselves to be ashamed of the gospel because someone doesn't agree with us, even if that person is apparently alert, intelligent, and well-intentioned. Don't falter because you can't explain it in his terminology, in his context.'"

We noticed her dad waiting for a reaction from us.

"That's just what we needed to hear!" Autumn said as she got up and gave her dad a hug. "Thanks so much."

I stood up. "Yeah, that was perfect."

I was hungry and ready to leave.

"Nick, could I have a word with you for just a minute before we leave?" her dad asked.

I panicked. What did he need to say to me that he couldn't say in front of Autumn? "Okay," I said, feeling nervous.

"I'll be in the car," Autumn said and left.

He took me into his office and we sat down, him behind a large desk, me in a padded armchair on the other side of the desk.

"I have enjoyed meeting you," he said. "Autumn has talked a great deal about the adventures you two are having."

"It's been good. Can I ask you a question?"

"Yes, of course."

"What have you learned from being a mayor?"

He had to think about it. "Okay, here it is. Do your best. Involve others in your decisions. Don't take flak personally. Very few people will ever tell you you're doing a good job. Basically, all you're going to get are complaints."

"Tough job."

"Yeah, it is. Also, if you're a mayor, you have to have a vision of what you want to accomplish. If you make all your decisions based on the situation at hand, you'll never get much done."

I remembered a concept from a business management class I had taken and asked, "So, did you come up with a formal vision statement?"

"Not at first, but I did after a few months on the job. One more thing, don't be afraid of boring people. You have to keep stressing what your vision is. And that means repetition. And that means it'll be boring to some people. That's not necessarily bad. You probably need to do the same thing in Dr. Penstock's class."

"Good idea. Thanks."

"Sure. Now can I ask you a few questions?"

"Sure. Fire away," I said with more confidence than I was feeling.

"What are you going to do after law school?"

"Work for my dad in his law firm."

"What sort of work will that be?"

"Mostly contracts, wills, estate planning agreements."

"What is your vision statement for that?"

"To make some money and provide for my family."

He shook his head. "That's good, but I think you ought to expand your vision a little. I recommend you make room in your life for some public service. That's where the rubber meets the road. Serve your community."

"I'll think about it."

He hesitated a moment before asking, "Does Autumn figure into your plans for the future?"

"Probably not. She talks a lot about a missionary she worked with on her mission. She and I are good friends though."

"I don't know you all that well, but you seem like a fine young man to me. This is none of my business, and you don't have to answer this, but I'll ask it anyway. Do you have a current temple recommend?"

"I do."

"Are you worthy of it?"

"Yes."

"Good for you." He paused. "Listen. Autumn is going to ask you what we've been talking about. If I know her, she'll be very angry if she finds out I've been asking about the possibility of the two of you eventually getting together. But here's the thing—being the only Mormon in her high school was very hard on her. I know she wanted to date, but there just weren't any candidates. As parents, our desire is that she find and marry a worthy Latter-day Saint man. I'm not saying you are the one for her. I'm just saying I'm glad she's met someone we can feel good about her being with. That's all."

While telling me this, he abandoned his big, football coach's voice. He stood up and came around to my side of the desk and took my hand in his big bear paw. As we shook hands I could see in his eyes how much he cared for his daughter.

"Just know, Nick, that Autumn's mother and I are glad she has found such a good friend."

After we got home and were getting ready to eat lunch, Autumn suggested that after we ate, we should begin our fast for the next day, which was Fast Sunday.

"Okay. What should we fast for?" I asked.

"I think we should petition Heavenly Father to help us in Penstock's class."

"Good idea."

Before I start fasting, I tend to eat everything in sight, like I may never eat anything again. At lunch Autumn noticed me pigging out but didn't say anything to me about it.

After lunch we told her parents what we were going to

do, excused ourselves from the table, went into the living room, knelt down, and prayed together.

When we stood up, she gave me a brief hug. "Thank you for doing this with me."

"It'll be good."

We ended up in the sunroom reading scriptures for forty-five minutes, and then we drove her car over to her ward meetinghouse, the only one in town. Her dad, being in the bishopric, had a key to the building.

She gave me a tour of the building, pointing out where she had attended Primary and where the Young Women met. We went into the chapel and she showed me where their family always sat in church.

Then she went behind the podium and played the piano. We even sang some hymns together.

While sitting next to each other on the piano bench, she asked, "So what did you and my dad talk about after I left?"

I remembered his warning and casually said, "Oh, he just wanted to give me some advice, you know, about life and school and being a lawyer."

"Is that all?"

"Pretty much."

"Did he say anything about . . . us?"

I didn't want to tell her he hoped we would eventually get together, so all I said was, "He told me how much he loves you."

That made her smile and seemed to satisfy her.

And then we went home.

We watched some church movies the rest of the night, and then at nine-thirty, her parents invited us for family prayer. After that, we separated for the night.

On Sunday morning I woke up at six-thirty with only one thought on my mind: *How can I ever not be with this girl?*

I had no answer to that question.

We went to church, came home, had lunch with her folks, loaded up her car, said our good-byes, and headed back to the real world.

I had two promptings from the Spirit: one was the feeling that Heavenly Father would help us as we tried to defend gospel truths in our class. The second prompting concerned Autumn: I felt like I was not to worry about the future but to do my best to help her any way I could.

It wasn't exactly what I wanted to hear, but I accepted it as coming from Father in Heaven.

Chapter Seven

Before class on Monday, Autumn and I decided that we would only participate in discussions in Penstock's class when we could present gospel principles. Also, we would present our explanations in terms of the gospel and do as President Packer suggested and "stay in context."

Our hope was that if we did that, perhaps someone in the class might feel the Spirit and someday be willing to listen to the missionaries.

On Monday, Penstock railed against capitalism. We sat there and said nothing. He seemed disappointed.

On Wednesday, he lectured to the class about his personal political views. Again, we didn't take the bait.

On Friday he brought his wife, Virginia, to class as a guest speaker. She asserted that Mormon women are dominated by their husbands and by the Church. She said that Mormon men subjugate their wives and keep them "barefoot and pregnant."

Autumn and I looked at each other. "I'll take this one," she said quietly.

"Okay. Good luck."

"Thanks."

She raised her hand, and Penstock got a big smile on his face. "You have a question or comment, Ms. Jones?"

Autumn stood up and moved to the aisle. "Yes, I do."

She refuted some of the comments that Mrs. Penstock had made, and then she began to quote from "The Family: A Proclamation to the World."

After a few seconds, Dr. Penstock interrupted her. "None of us care to hear you preach. Sit down."

Virginia Penstock said to him, "No, let her continue."

"Thank you," Autumn said to Virginia. "I'll just be a few more minutes."

When she had finished reading the entire Proclamation, Autumn looked down at her notes. "Just one more thought from Gordon B. Hinckley, a man who, when he was alive, we sustained as a prophet, seer, and revelator. He said, 'To you men and women of great influence, you who preside in the cities of the nation, to you I say that it will cost far less to reform our schools, to teach the virtues of good citizenship, than it will to go on building and maintaining costly jails and prisons. . . . But there is another institution of even greater importance than the schools. It is the home. I believe that no nation can rise higher than the strength of its families.'"

"Are you done yet?" Penstock grumbled.

Autumn ignored the question. "Mrs. Penstock, I know that God lives. He is our Father in Heaven. We knew Him before we were born. Jesus Christ is our Savior. Through Him all mankind can be saved. I also know that Joseph

Smith was a Prophet of God. I know this because God has revealed it to me through the power of the Holy Ghost, as He will to all those who seek to know His will."

Autumn sat down.

Dr. Penstock glared at her, then in a chiding tone, raised both hands in the air and chanted, "Hallelujah! Hallelujah! Pass the plate!"

"Thomas, shame on you! Quit badgering this girl," Mrs. Penstock said.

His face turned a bright red. He didn't like being corrected by his wife, especially in his classroom in front of his students. "You can go home now," he said to Virginia.

"Yes, I can, and I will."

Seconds after Virginia Penstock left the classroom, Autumn pulled a copy of the Book of Mormon out of her backpack and ran out of the classroom.

When Autumn returned ten minutes later, she leaned close to me and whispered, "She accepted it!"

"That's great!" I whispered.

The rest of the class period was predictable and boring.

After class, I turned to Autumn. "What did you say when you gave her the Book of Mormon?" I asked.

"I told her I knew it was true and promised her that if she would read it and pray about it, she would know it too. She didn't say anything for a while, and then she looked me in the eye and said, 'I will read it.'"

We were so happy as we made our way to the library. As soon as we were in our private study room, Autumn said, "We need to pray."

We knelt down, and she said she wanted to offer the prayer.

She thanked Heavenly Father for His help, and she prayed for Mrs. Penstock. Halfway through, her voice sort of cracked, and I opened my eyes and looked at her. Tears of happiness were streaming down her face.

After the prayer, we stood up and looked at each other. "You're amazing," I said softly.

"Not me. Heavenly Father is, though."

"Yeah, I know."

I reached for her hand. She must have thought we were going to shake hands. But we didn't. I just held her hand.

I got kind of emotional as I said, "You know, I'm glad I met you. Before, I was such a coward. Without your courage, I never would have dared challenge someone like Penstock. Thanks for being such a great example."

"I'm learning from you as well," she said.

That made me smile.

"What's with the silly grin on your face?" she asked.

"Nice job saying *as well*."

"I have no idea what you mean."

"*As well* sounds more intelligent than saying 'I'm learning from you too.'"

Just then Keifer came into the room.

"It's Ms. Keifer!" Autumn said excitedly.

"And she didn't catch us frolicking!" I said behind my hand.

Autumn suppressed a laugh and then turned to welcome our visitor. "Good morning! What can we do for you today?"

Keifer frowned. "Why do you always say that?"

"Say what?" Autumn asked.

"'What can we do for you today?' Nobody I've ever worked with here says that to me."

"We want to help out if we can," Autumn said.

Keifer sagged onto a chair and wiped at her eyes with a tissue.

"Is something wrong?" Autumn asked.

"Circulation is down," she said, wiping a tear from her wrinkled face. "We buy books all the time, but few are ever checked out." She sighed. "Everyone is doing online research."

Autumn patted the woman's hand. "This is hard for you, isn't it?"

Keifer nodded and then blew her nose.

At the rate she was going, she was going to need more tissues. I went into the office area in the next room and rummaged around the empty desks until I found a box of tissues and returned to our study area.

Keifer shook her head. "If this doesn't turn around, our budget for new books is going to be cut drastically." She burst into tears and reached for a fresh tissue. "What kind of a library will this be with no new books?" she blubbered.

"More like a museum that nobody ever visits," I said.

Autumn glared at me. I shrugged and placed the box of tissues in front of Keifer. She dropped her head onto her folded arms and sobbed.

Her grief seemed so unwarranted. I couldn't take it any longer. I moved to the far end of the table and sat down, leaving Autumn to comfort the distraught woman.

While I was waiting, I did some online searches on my laptop. A few minutes later I began writing down some things the library could do to increase the circulation of books.

I could tell Keifer was feeling better when she asked Autumn if she might have "a tiny bit of chocolate."

"Nick, did you bring chocolate today?" Autumn asked.

I joined them with a small bag of chocolate I'd picked up that morning on my way to campus.

Before long Keifer was regaling us with stories from her early days as a reference librarian. Autumn at least seemed to enjoy it.

"Nick, what were you working on while Ms. Keifer and I were talking?"

"Oh, not much. Just a few ideas of ways we might be able to increase circulation."

"Could you tell us what they are?" Autumn asked.

"Yeah, I guess. They're just a few ideas that came to mind, that's all." I handed Autumn the page of scribbled notes.

She looked them over then said, "Ms. Keifer, if you're interested, I could read these to you, and you can tell us if there are any that seem promising."

She put up her hand. "Please, it's not necessary for you to call me Ms. Keifer. My friends call me Marian."

Autumn smiled. "Okay, we'll call you that from now on, won't we, Nick?"

"Yes, we will," I said, privately thinking there was no way I could call her Marian the Librarian and keep a straight face.

Autumn read my first idea. "Buy more e-books so students can check out books and read them online." She stopped and looked at me. "Is that even possible?"

"It is. In fact, the library here already has two hundred books that can be checked out online."

We looked over to Keifer for her response. "Oh, that was done by someone we hired just out of college. He insisted we needed to do it. Some of us were reluctant, but we did let him start a pilot project. Shortly after he'd bought some online books, we had another budget cut and we had to let him go."

"After he left, did you promote the idea of online books?" I asked.

"Not really. Some of us don't really agree with the idea," Keifer said. "We think students should come to the library and check out an actual book."

"The way I see it," I said, "if your budget is based on the number of people who check out books each year, then an online checkout is as valid as someone checking out an actual book. Why should you care how students do it?"

Keifer sighed. "A book is a wonderful thing. You can take it with you and read it anywhere you want. I love the smell of a book. I love to turn the pages. It becomes my friend while I'm reading it."

I shrugged. "It's a bunch of words thrown together. I'd much rather get an e-book from my apartment than have to hike here to get it and then hike back."

Keifer closed her eyes, slowly shook her head, and sighed. "All I want is for people to love books like I have all my life."

I looked over at Autumn for any suggestions she might have. She just shrugged her shoulders.

I had to say it. "With all due respect, Ms. Keifer, have you ever considered the possibility that, because you're not actively promoting e-books, you may be in some small way contributing to the reason why the library has lost funding?"

I might as well have slapped her. She ran out of the room in tears.

Autumn looked over at me, shook her head, and then took off after Keifer.

I waited for an hour. I was afraid Autumn would give up on me. I wanted her to come back and talk to me. If she wanted me to apologize to Keifer, I'd do it. I'd do anything she asked me to do to make things right again between us.

While I waited, I came up with a few other things Autumn and I could do to help increase circulation.

Just as I was about to leave, Autumn and Keifer returned.

I stood up. "Ms. Keifer, what I said was totally inappropriate. I sincerely apologize. Please forgive me."

She wouldn't look at me, but she did nod.

"Marian has agreed to let us see what we can do to increase circulation," Autumn said.

"Thank you," I said.

She nodded but still avoided eye contact with me.

"Okay, let me run some more ideas past you," I said. We all sat down.

"Maybe we could have some more chocolate now," Autumn suggested.

Keifer shook her head.

"Let's do," I said, passing the bag of chocolate to Autumn, who took two pieces and set one on the conference table in front of Keifer. Keifer didn't even look at it.

"Please tell us your ideas, Nick," Autumn said.

"First idea: We promote the online books the library has already purchased. We feature them on the library Web site and with posters in the library. If you can, I'd also suggest you buy more online books."

Keifer sighed. "To me this seems like giving up."

"Marian," I said, breaking my vow to never call her by her first name, "I totally understand why you feel that way."

"I will just have to trust that you two know what you're doing," she said.

"Thank you," I said. "Second idea: we get a mobile cart we can take anywhere on campus. We pile some books on it, take it to where students are. Get them to look them over, and check out the books online."

"How would you do that?" Autumn asked.

"We could use a student's ID card like a credit card, run it through an online reader that checks it out to them, then hand 'em the book. If a movie has been made from the book, we could package them together and check out both the DVD and the book. Some students would watch the movie first and then read the book."

Keifer sighed and then nodded her head. "I will see if I can get permission to do a pilot project."

"How long will that take?" I asked.

"Three or four months."

"Autumn and I don't have that much time," I said. "We're both graduating in May. Look, let's just do it. If it works out, you can tell 'em what we did. If not, you can look for some other idea to try."

She nodded. "How much do you think it will cost?" Keifer asked.

"I'd say less than a thousand dollars. Most of it for a laptop and setting up online checkout procedures."

Keifer nodded. "Okay, go ahead with that then. I have a budget account I can take it out of."

The next day, a Saturday, Autumn and I met at the

library to work on the mobile book cart idea. Since the next day was Valentine's Day, I gave her some flowers and asked her to have dinner with me at a restaurant.

"Okay, but I feel bad I didn't even get you a card."

"It's okay. Don't worry about it."

We had an okay time together, but I think she was a little worried that someday she'd hurt my feelings because of Elder Wonderful.

Instead of avoiding the subject, I asked her about how things were going between her and her missionary.

"There's not much to report. We write once a week."

"So in your letters do you talk about a possible future together?" I asked.

"No, not at all! He's totally focused on his mission. He tells me about the people he's teaching and about the success he's having. And also, each week we agree to read the same twenty pages in the Book of Mormon and in our letters tell each other what we've learned. He always brings up such interesting points I've never thought of before. His dad has been teaching an institute class for years, so Christopher—I finally asked him his first name—has benefited from what his dad has taught during family home evening. I'm learning so much."

I don't know why, but that depressed me. *Who can compete with that?* I thought.

I took her home after we'd eaten, gave her a hug, and returned to my apartment, where I spent an hour studying the scriptures, looking desperately for some insights that would impress Autumn. But everything I came up with I figured that Autumn, because she served a mission, would already know.

For the next two weeks, we worked on developing ideas to increase library circulation. After getting Keifer's approval for the design of our mobile library cart, we took the drawings to the carpentry shop on campus and asked them to make it. Also, we found a student who already worked in the library to work on the checkout protocol. He also agreed to do weekly e-mails to students about virtual books they could check out online. That alone boosted circulation significantly.

Because of everything we were doing for the library, Autumn and I also started to work together at night. Often we'd eat dinner together on campus and then go to our office in the library to work. Sometime between ten-thirty and eleven at night, I'd walk her to her apartment. We'd talk for a while, share a kiss or two at her door, and then say good night. We both carefully avoided talking about the future.

We scheduled the grand opening of the library cart project for Wednesday, March 10. We were given access to the theatre department's costume storage room. Autumn would be Scarlett O'Hara, and I would be Rhett Butler. Using library funds, we purchased a poster that advertised the movie *Gone with the Wind*. We tacked it onto the library cart and filled the cart with classic American novels. Each novel was bundled with a DVD of the movie that had been made from the book.

On the first day, we headed to a high-traffic area in the student union building. At first people just walked past us, so we began acting out a scene from the movie. People stopped to watch us. When we were done, we invited them to check out a book/DVD bundle and share it with someone special.

We also had a poster on our cart that listed books and resources students could access online. That seemed to be welcome news to many students.

Within two hours we'd helped students check out twenty book/DVD bundles. The next day we checked out ten more.

When Keifer learned of our success, she was ecstatic. The next day she brought us chocolate.

A week later, on St. Patrick's Day, just after we finished studying together for the night, Autumn asked if we could stay in the library for a few more minutes. "I need some advice," she said.

We sat down next to each other at the conference table.

"When I got home last night, I had a letter from, uh . . . Elder Bonneville."

"What'd he say?" I asked, trying not to sound too bitter.

"Mostly mission news. He also said that he would be reporting his mission the third Sunday in April. He invited me to come to Utah, stay with his folks, and hear him speak in sacrament meeting. He said his folks would pay my way."

"So, are you going to go?" I asked.

"I haven't answered his letter yet. What do you think I should tell him?"

I was mad. "Look, you tell that clown that if he wants to see you after his mission, then he can just jump on a plane and come out here! How could you even consider going out there just because he asks you! Don't you have any self-respect?"

"When we were in the same district, we worked well together. We respect each other."

"So, how does he catch a break, and I don't?"

"You're jealous, aren't you?"

"Jealous? Me? Why would I be jealous? In a couple of months we'll graduate and this whole stupid thing will all be over." I didn't want to talk about it anymore. "Look, you do whatever you want, okay?"

That night at her door, we hugged, but when I tried to kiss her, she turned her head away.

"Anything wrong?" I asked.

"I'm just a little confused about things now."

"Yeah, sure."

"What about you? Are you okay?" she asked me.

"Honestly, I'm out-of-my-mind jealous. You know what? I'd better just go."

"We can still hug."

I sighed. "Yeah, sure, hugs are good." I hugged her for like a second and then said good night.

A few days later she told me that she'd decided that I was right. She wouldn't be going out to Utah to hear Elder Bonneville report on his mission.

"That's good," I said.

"He wants to come out for my graduation, though."

"That's better. He should be the one who is proactive, not you."

I couldn't read the expression on her face as she said, "Nick, why is he writing me?"

I didn't think I'd have to explain it to her; it was pretty clear to me. "It's very simple. The guy is obviously a goal-setter. He plans ahead. He knows marriage is important, and right now you're someone he would consider marrying." I tried not to sound bitter, but it was hard.

She nodded.

"How do you feel about him?" I asked.

"I guess the same way he feels about me. I admire him."

"Would you ever get married to a guy just because you admire him?"

"No, of course not."

"Good."

"There's something else," she said.

"What?"

"He says he's had the impression that he and I should get married," she said.

I threw up my hands in frustration. "Oh, give me a break, okay? You're not so naïve to just accept his word on that, are you?"

"No, of course not. It does make me think about it, though. Like, what if it's true?"

"Have *you* had any promptings in that direction?"

"No."

"Well, that's got to tell you something then, right?"

She nodded. "You're absolutely right," she said.

That night, at the door to her apartment, I tried to kiss her, but she turned her head away again. "Not tonight."

"I understand." I stepped away from her. "We can, you know, put that part on hold. If you want."

She nodded. "Let me think about it, okay? Well, good night."

"Good night. See you tomorrow."

On my walk back to my apartment, I felt awful.

The next week she didn't hear from Elder Bonneville, even though she'd written him a letter. I figured she was just going to let things play out after he came home from his mission because one night after studying together at the library as I was about to leave her at the door, she cleared her throat. "Don't go yet," she said.

"Okay."

She closed her eyes and lowered her head. I could tell she was uncomfortable. "This is awkward and embarrassing, but, uh, would you please kiss me?"

I felt a big smile cross my face. "I'd be more than happy to do that. Anytime, actually."

She shook her head. "Please don't talk," she said.

And so I kissed her.

"I've missed that so much," she said softly.

"Me too."

"But of course, in a way, I'm disappointed in myself," she said.

"Why's that?" I asked.

"I don't know."

"We haven't done anything wrong. You do know that, right?"

"I know. So it's okay if we . . ."

"Yes, as long as we're following the rules we set up."

"Thank you." She sighed. "This is embarrassing. I've never been . . . uh . . . *needy* before, but apparently I am. I'm not sure what to make of that."

"Hey, don't worry about it. It's okay."

"It's not just about kissing, either. It's also how you treat me, how much fun we have when we're together, how we're able to work together. All of those things."

"That will pass once Elder Wonderful gets back from his mission."

She scowled at me. "His last name is Bonneville."

I shrugged. "I know. Sorry. You're right. I'm not being fair to him. I guess I'm just jealous."

"There's a part of me that's glad you're jealous of him."

I guess it was that night that I finally had to admit to myself that I'd fallen in love with her. I didn't see how I could tell her though. I was afraid she'd freak out and do something noble, like tell me she didn't think we should see each other anymore.

Also, graduation day was only two months away. My dad wanted me to work in his law office in the summer. Autumn was hoping to work in some orphanage in Ecuador. Just like her, right? And when she got back from that, chances were I'd be out of the picture.

And so, like it or not, two months was all the time I had left with her.

Chapter Eight

The semester seemed to fly past. In Penstock's class we did our best to stand up for what we believed in, and he did his best to sabotage our efforts.

On the first Friday in April, one of Penstock's clone graduate students opened the door at the beginning of class and announced, "No class today. Go home."

"All right!" someone in the back row shouted. There was a mad rush to get out of the room.

Autumn and I went down to the front of the room to talk to the graduate student.

"No class today. Go home," he repeated.

"Yeah, we got that part," I said. "So what's up with Dr. Penstock?"

The student didn't seem to understand what I meant. "Up?"

"Where is he?" Autumn asked.

"Hospital. No class. Go home." He put his clipboard under his arm and walked crisply toward the door.

We followed him. "Why's he in the hospital?" I asked.

"Shot."

"He's in the hospital for a shot?" I asked.

"No, he shot . . . with gun . . . on street."

"He was shot on the street?"

"Shot on street, yes."

"What hospital?"

The graduate student looked at his clipboard and shrugged his shoulders. "No class today. Go home." And then he left.

We called the dean's office, and they told us which hospital Penstock was at. We drove there in Autumn's car to see him.

We found him in the intensive care unit. The nurse wouldn't let us into his room, but we could see him and his wife through the window. Penstock had on an oxygen mask and was sleeping.

As soon as she noticed us, Mrs. Penstock came out to the nurses' station. I was surprised when she hugged Autumn and then took me by the hand and held it. "I'm so glad you both came."

"What happened?" Autumn asked.

"He was waiting for his bus. The police said a witness told them that a man started yelling at the woman who was with him. They argued, and then he struck her across the face with his hand. When Thomas tried to intervene, the man pushed him away and struck the woman again. Thomas tried to stop him, but the man went crazy. He took out a gun, shot Thomas in the stomach, and ran off. The police are still looking for him."

She turned to look at her husband through the window

and cleared her throat. "They say it's serious. I don't know what I'll do if . . ." She couldn't say anymore.

"I am so sorry," Autumn said.

"They operated on him last night and removed the bullet. It seemed to miss his major organs. The thing they're most worried about now is infection. So it could be worse. But Thomas is diabetic and that can always complicate things . . . so naturally I'm worried."

"Of course."

"Do Mormons ever pray over the sick?" she asked Autumn.

"We do."

"Would you do that for me, please?"

Autumn turned to me. "Nick here has the power to bless the sick. We call that power from God the priesthood."

"Will you do that for me?" Mrs. Penstock quickly asked.

I nodded. "Yes, of course. We usually have at least two. If it's okay, I'd like to call our missionaries and have them come help me."

She nodded. "Thank you."

I called the mission office and asked them to send two elders to help me administer to someone at the hospital. They said they'd be right over.

Then I needed to convince the nurse to let us go in to give Penstock a blessing. I was lucky. The nurse wasn't LDS, but she had a sister who was, so she knew something about administering to the sick. She said we could go in but only for a short while. The three of us would have to wash our hands and each wear a sanitary smock, which she got for us.

While we were waiting for the elders to arrive,

Mrs. Penstock said to Autumn, "I've been reading that book you gave me."

"The Book of Mormon?" Autumn said.

"Yes."

"You have?" I asked.

"Yes, of course. I said I would, and I make it a point to keep my promises."

"What do you think about it?" Autumn asked.

"I'm not sure yet." She paused. "I will say one thing, though. It deserves more respect than my minister gave it when I told him I was reading it. After he finished trashing all things Mormon, I asked him if he'd ever read the Book of Mormon. Turns out he hadn't. Can you get me another copy to give him?"

"I'm sure the elders will have one in their car," I assured her.

The two elders finally arrived. They couldn't have been more different from each other. Elder Watson was tall and lanky and had a cowboy twang. His companion, Elder Brown, was soft-spoken and seemed embarrassed by everything Elder Watson said.

Elder Watson got right to the point. He shook Mrs. Penstock's hand and said, "So your husband got shot, right?"

"Yes."

"I got shot once too. Hunting accident. My brother did it." He chuckled. "At least he said it was an accident. Well, don't you worry none, okay?"

Elder Brown also shook her hand and mumbled something I couldn't hear.

Elder Watson turned to me. "Okay, chief, you tell us what you want us to do here."

I thought it would be important for Mrs. Penstock to hear what was said. "Elder Watson, will you anoint? And I'll seal the anointing."

We washed our hands, put on our smocks, and were allowed into Penstock's room. The elders and I stood around the bed.

Penstock opened his eyes and panicked. "Virginia?" he called out.

She stepped to the head of his bed and said, "Yes, Thomas?"

"Who are these people?"

"Well, you remember Nick from class, right? And these other two are missionaries from the Mormon Church. They're going to pray over you."

"I don't want anyone praying over me. Tell them to leave," he ordered.

"I invited them, Thomas. You need God's help. Just close your eyes and be quiet."

He looked up at us and swore.

"Thomas, behave yourself! I will not have you dying on me, is that clear?"

He sighed and rolled his eyes.

"We've got the doctors doing everything they can do," Mrs. Penstock said to her husband. "Now it's time to ask for God's help."

"Oh, so now you're an expert on God, right?" he asked sarcastically.

"We'll talk about this later, Thomas. Keep quiet so they can do this."

He nodded and closed his eyes, not out of reverence but because he wanted no part in any of this.

And so we proceeded. At first it felt awkward, giving a blessing to a man who didn't believe in God and who resented our even being there. Then during the blessing I heard myself saying that Penstock would recover quickly with no permanent effects from the bullet wound. I also said he'd live a long, useful life and that he'd be a great support to his wife after she was baptized and that he would, in time, take her to the temple where their marriage would continue into the eternities.

When I finished, Penstock opened his eyes. I expected him to get after me, but he didn't. He just looked at me and nodded. Soon after that he fell asleep.

Outside the room, Mrs. Penstock gave me a hug and thanked me. The elders said they'd check back the next day to see how Dr. Penstock was doing. Virginia asked if they could bring her another copy of the Book of Mormon for her minister. They said they'd be more than happy to do that. And then they left.

As Autumn and I were leaving the hospital, she reached for my hand. "Thank you for being worthy to receive the promptings of the Spirit."

I had given several blessings while serving as a missionary, but this was a new experience for me. I was still stunned by what I had been moved to promise Penstock, and I didn't know what to say. So I just nodded my head.

When we reached campus, we went to the library, knelt in prayer and prayed for Penstock and his wife. Then we began to prepare for our next library cart excursion. We sat down and brainstormed for a while on what the theme would be. Whatever the theme, we had to be able to come up with a cartful of books and movies.

We were in the middle of tossing out ideas when I stopped and said to her, "There is no one I'd rather work with than you."

She smiled. "Thank you, Nick. We do work well together, don't we?"

"We're off on another adventure, right? Just like in Scooby-Doo."

"Right, off for another adventure. That's us, for sure."

I thought of telling her I loved her, but I didn't. I was afraid it would have gotten in the way and made us self-conscious, that she'd pull back, and I'd lose what I had with her.

And, of course, by now there were just six weeks until we'd both graduate and go our separate ways.

That night I woke up at two in the morning, worrying that I had promised too much in the blessing I had given Dr. Penstock. I'd promised him he'd suffer no ill effects of being shot in the stomach. How could I say that? I'd said that Mrs. Penstock would get baptized and that her husband would support her. How did I know that? And the promise that they would be married in the temple? Where did that come from?

Even though it was two-thirty in the morning, I ended up calling Autumn. She picked up almost immediately and acted like it was no inconvenience at all for her.

She listened to me for a long time as I told her what my concerns were, and then she asked one question: "Did you feel the Spirit when you gave the blessing?"

"I think so."

"That's all that counts, isn't it? It's okay if you're second-guessing yourself now. Just remember how you felt when you gave the blessing."

"Thank you. So it'll be okay?"

"It will."

"I'm sorry for calling so late."

"That's what friends are for. If it were me, I'd call you. So it all works out, right?"

She had made me feel so much better. Maybe it was the sense of relief I felt, or maybe I was just so tired, but I blurted out, "I love you."

There was a long pause. "I love you too, Nick. You're the best friend I've ever had. Oh, I keep forgetting to ask you. Would you like to watch conference with me tomorrow?"

"Yeah, I would."

"In the library?"

"Yeah."

"See you then."

We hung up, and I soon fell asleep.

Chapter Nine

The next morning, I worried that I'd crossed the line in telling her I loved her. I was worried she'd say we shouldn't see each other anymore. I didn't want to do that though. I kidded myself that all I wanted was to enjoy what little time we had together before we graduated. But that wasn't true. I wasn't ready to give her up at all. How was I going to arrange that? I hadn't a clue.

Lucky for me, she didn't mention the "I love you" thing when we met at the library. I hoped she had just chalked it up to me being sleepy.

We had a great day watching conference. Autumn had brought sandwiches for lunch, so we had a picnic on the conference table. It was good.

Saturday night after the priesthood session, I bought take-out so we'd have something to eat the next day between sessions.

On Sunday, we watched conference in the nearest stake

building, and then we ate the food I'd gotten the night before.

After we ate, we called Mrs. Penstock to ask how her husband was doing.

She told us he seemed to be doing a little better. Autumn asked if she'd had a chance to watch conference. She said, "No, tell me what happened." So we took turns telling her what the highlights were for us.

And then we watched the afternoon session.

It was a perfect day except that while we were eating, Autumn shared some insights from Second Nephi that Elder Wonderful had shared with her in a recent letter. I had to admit they were valid insights. I just wished I'd had some of my own.

On Monday we spent some time in the theater department's costume storeroom picking out what we'd wear for our next Library on Wheels Day. This time we'd chosen "Baseball Books and Movies" as our theme.

We found some baseball uniforms. "I wonder if these pants would fit me," she said.

"Probably."

"Turn around and close your eyes," she told me.

I did. "I can't believe you're changing in my presence."

"I trust you. Besides, it would take too long to find a restroom."

"The things I put up with," I complained while she changed.

"Okay, you can turn around."

I looked at what she was wearing. "It looks okay."

"Yeah, it does. Do you want to see if those pants fit you?"

"Yes, but I'm certainly not going to try them on with you here."

"I promise I won't look."

"I just can't do this, okay? It would be too weird, that's all. Is it asking too much for us both to just keep our clothes on when we're together?"

That made her laugh out loud. "I'm so glad nobody heard that!"

When we finished our work at the library, we went to the student union to get a snack.

"I got another letter from Elder Bonneville," she said.

"How's he doing?"

"Great. They divided one of the stakes in the mission last weekend, so he got to meet two general authorities." She told me their names.

"That's always a good experience," I said.

"And they had a mission conference Friday morning with both of the general authorities. Elder Bonneville conducted the meeting. Afterward, they told him he'd done an excellent job."

"I'm sure he did. Elder Bonneville is a great missionary, isn't he?"

"Yes, he is. One of the finest."

"I'm sure."

• • •

While Penstock was recovering from his gunshot wound, one of the graduate students taught us. Basically, each class he asked if there were any questions on the reading. There never were because we all knew we'd never understand any answer he might give. He then gave a multiple-choice quiz that could be found at the end of each chapter in the text-book, wrote the next reading assignment on the board, and then dismissed the class. The whole thing usually took less than ten minutes.

On Friday, April 16, Penstock returned to class in a wheelchair, accompanied by his wife. She greeted us warmly before class and asked if she could sit with us. We noticed him glaring at us.

"Your husband seems mad about something," Autumn said.

"Since Thomas has been home, the elders have been coming to our house to teach me. He's not happy with that, and he blames you two for what's happening."

"Virginia, get up here. It's time to start!" Penstock grumbled.

She nodded and hurried to be with him in case he needed any help in the class.

He wasted no time getting back at us. "I have only quizzes for the class for the past two weeks, so I've decided to give you a test that will count for ten percent of your final grade. There is just one question: State the reasons you have for favoring same-gender marriage. You have fifteen minutes. Begin now."

Autumn and I looked at each other and then both of us raised our hands.

"This is an exam, not a discussion," he said to us.

"But we don't favor same-gender marriage," Autumn said.

"Then I guess you either fake it or flunk the exam."

"How about if we give reasons why we don't favor same-gender marriage?" Autumn suggested.

"You mean reasons like hatred and bigotry?"

"No. We will give valid reasons," she said.

"Don't even bother. I won't read your paper, and you will get an automatic F."

"All right then," she said. "We'll do what we need to do, and you do what you feel you need to do."

I stood up. "I would just like to read from your syllabus about the part that talks about free and open—"

He banged his fist on the table. "Mr. Baxter, this is not a discussion! This is a test! And if you two say anything else, I will fail both of you for the entire class."

We sat down and began writing.

Mrs. Penstock left her husband and came to sit down next to us. In a voice loud enough for everyone to hear, she said, "Since you two are going to get an F anyway, how about we leave and have a nice lunch?"

We nodded and stood up to leave.

"Virginia, you come back here! I need your help."

"Sorry, I've made other plans."

"I demand you come up here and be with me, not with them!"

She let him have it. "You demand? Who do you think you are, talking to me that way? And another thing, who made you the dictator of the world anyway? I am not happy with what I'm seeing in you lately, Thomas."

"And you're blaming me for that? You spend hours being brainwashed by those Mormon missionaries! It's like you've lost your mind! It was bad enough when you read the Bible, but now you're reading the Book of Mormon, too! You want to end up like these two so-called students here?"

"Actually, I would like that very much. They defend

themselves in spite of you trying to tear down the faith of anyone who believes in God." She turned to the class. "Quit writing for a minute. I need to say something to you students."

"Keep writing, or I'll flunk all of you!" Penstock warned.

"Really, Thomas? If you do that, don't you suppose some of them might complain to the dean? I would personally encourage them to do that. Do you really want to fight that battle when you're so near retirement?"

He didn't answer the question.

Mrs. Penstock continued. "I want you students to know that I am reading the Book of Mormon, and I believe it is true and that its teachings are from God. I have had many questions throughout my life about religion, and now I am getting some answers to those questions. If you ever have a chance to learn from the missionaries of the Mormon Church, I suggest you do it."

Penstock, his face red with anger, pointed at Autumn and me. "You two are no longer welcome in this class! I don't want to ever see you again, do you understand?"

"You wouldn't even be alive if it weren't for the elders and Nick praying over you," Mrs. Penstock shot back. And then she turned to us. "Let's go. If you're not welcome here, I'm not welcome either."

We walked out of the class.

As we left the building, Mrs. Penstock broke the tension by saying cheerfully, "He looks good, don't you think?"

"Oh, yeah, for sure," I said with a smile. "I'd say he's pretty much back to his old self."

The three of us laughed.

"Let's have lunch," Mrs. Penstock said.

"We usually work in the library right after your husband's class. We're volunteers," Autumn said. "Would you like to come and see what we're working on?"

"I would be delighted. Let me just turn my cell phone off first. I don't want to be interrupted."

"What if your husband calls?"

"Yes, what if he does?" She turned off her cell phone.

"He might need you to help him," Autumn said.

"He has graduate students."

We were working on our plans for the next mobile library cart project, which would have a "What I Like to Do in the Summer" theme.

The three of us went to the costume shop and found some costumes that fit the theme, and then returned to our conference room in the library.

"You have this room all to yourself?" Mrs. Penstock asked when we first entered.

"Yeah. It's a great place to study," I said.

"Also," Autumn said, "one of our traditions is to have some chocolate while we're here. Nick picks it up every morning on his walk to campus. What have you got for us today, Nick?"

"A dark chocolate and almond mix. It's one of our favorites." I took a pair of scissors and cut the bag open so we could all share the chocolate.

"You two are quite the pair! Are you dating?"

"Not exactly. Mostly we're just very good friends," Autumn said. "We work amazingly well together, and we have a great time doing it."

I nodded. "After we graduate, I'll go back home and work in my dad's law office. And in the fall, I'll start Harvard Law

School. But that all depends on my getting an A in your husband's class—something that's looking pretty doubtful at this point."

She didn't say anything to reassure me but instead turned to Autumn. "What about you, Autumn? What will you do after you graduate?"

She paused. "I'm not sure yet."

"I pray for you both every day."

"You do? Why?"

"I thank God for you coming into my life. Without you two, I would have never had a chance to learn about the Church and about the Restoration. I'm very grateful."

Autumn and I traded glances. Her eyes sent the message, *I guess we have done some good here.*

"You two are so fortunate to have found each other," Mrs. Penstock said. She hesitated, then turned to me. "Nick, I was wondering if you would consent to baptizing me. When I asked the elders about it, they said it would be okay if you are willing. We've set a date for a week from tomorrow."

I was totally blown away. I didn't know she was that close to being baptized. "Well, yeah. If that is what you want, I would love to do that."

"Thank you."

"Have you told your husband yet?" Autumn asked.

"No, but I will today."

Autumn hugged Mrs. Penstock. I went to shake her hand, but she pulled me in and gave me a hug. "If we had ever had children, I would have wanted them to be just like you two. Your parents must be very proud of you."

"Thank you," we both said.

She led us to a small boutique restaurant just off campus that only fine arts majors and their professors went to.

At Mrs. Penstock's recommendation, I ordered a chicken-and-cranberry sandwich on caraway rye bread with a glass of French carbonated water.

It took forever to get our food. When it finally came, I was surprised at how small the sandwich was. I had to pace myself so I didn't finish eating before Autumn and Mrs. Penstock. I promised myself that as soon as I was free, I'd get myself a Big Mac and fries.

As we made our way back to campus, Mrs. Penstock said, "May we have one more piece of chocolate for dessert? And then I'd like to see how Thomas is doing. If I might, I'll bring him a piece of chocolate. If he's reasonable, he can have it, but if not, I'll eat it myself."

A few minutes later we found Penstock in his office with his door open.

"We're back!" Mrs. Penstock said with a big smile.

"Where have you been?" he snapped.

"Well, first we went to the library. Did you know that Nick and Autumn are library volunteers? They're doing a marvelous job! And then we went out for lunch. We've had a wonderful time together."

He glared at Autumn and me. "I want you two out of my sight! You are no longer enrolled in my class."

"You can't do that, Thomas," Mrs. Penstock said.

"Why not?"

"If you do, I will personally accompany them to the dean's office and show them how to file a complaint against you."

"They already know how to do that," he said bitterly. "I

don't want you to be with those Mormons anymore. I do not want them in my house. I do not want them indoctrinating you."

"I'm sorry you feel that way, but as a matter of fact, I will be getting baptized next Saturday. I've asked Nick to baptize me. After that, I will be going to church every Sunday. You're always welcome to come with me. I think it would do you good."

He struggled to stand up. "That's it! This marriage is over!"

I was astonished at her reaction. He had just declared he wanted a divorce, and she didn't seem the least upset. Instead she said with a laugh, "Oh, Thomas, you don't really mean that. But if that's the way you truly feel, I'll box up all your things and put them in the garage for you to pick up. I know how busy you are and how much energy it takes to browbeat your students."

Talk about awkward. I started backing out of the room. "You know what? We probably should be going now."

Mrs. Penstock turned her attention to Autumn and me. "I'll come help you at the library in the morning," she said. "What time would you like me to be there?"

"Ten o'clock would be good," I said.

"See you then. Oh, and thanks for the chocolate." She put the piece of chocolate she'd saved for her husband into her mouth.

We were relieved to get away from them.

Autumn suggested we go back to the library and pray for the Penstocks. And so we did.

She offered the prayer. It was good.

Chapter Ten

As promised, Mrs. Penstock showed up at ten the next morning, but her husband, still in a wheelchair, came with her.

After greeting us warmly, Mrs. Penstock said, "Thomas wants to speak to you both this morning." She turned to her husband. "I'll be waiting by the elevator. When you're ready to go, have Nick come get me, okay?"

He nodded, and Mrs. Penstock left.

"I have come to apologize," he said softly.

Autumn and I were both in shock. "Oh," Autumn replied.

He looked around the room. "This is where you study?"

"Yes."

"I wish I'd had a place to study like this when I was a student."

"Yes, we like it very much."

"How did you get it?"

"We're library volunteers."

"Good for you." He yawned. "Sorry. Virginia and I were up most of the night talking. You saw the worst side of us yesterday. I know it's mostly my fault. Thank goodness she's so levelheaded. She's always found a way to cajole me out of my irrational tirades."

"You're not going to get divorced, then?" Autumn asked.

That was the first time I'd heard Dr. Penstock laugh. It wasn't a big laugh though. More like a snort. "No, we're not going to end our marriage. But we are going to see a marriage counselor and see what we can do to patch things up. The one thing she insisted on was that I apologize to you both, and so that's why I'm here today."

This was a whole new Dr. Penstock. Autumn and I just stared at him dumbly, wondering where this was going to go.

"You two study in here every day?"

"Yes," Autumn said.

"And you're the only students who are ever here?"

"Yes, that's right."

He rolled his wheelchair toward the fireplace. "Have you ever had a fire in here?"

"No, we haven't," I said. "We weren't sure we could do it without someone seeing smoke coming out of the building and calling the fire department. The thing is, since we're using this as our own private study area, someone in the administration might object and kick us out."

"Of course, the library staff knows we're here," Autumn quickly offered. "We signed up to be volunteers, so they let us stay." She paused. "We're just not sure the president of the university would approve of us being here."

He laughed lightly again. "Knowing him, I would definitely say that's true."

116

There was a pile of old textbooks in the corner of the room. Dr. Penstock noticed one of them and asked me to bring it to him, which I did.

He held it in his hand. "This was a textbook in one of my classes. Even as a student, I always knew I wanted to be a college professor. What a great job. I wanted to open up my students' minds to new thoughts. I wanted them to go through a process of discovery that would change them for the rest of their lives."

He gave the book back to me. "Last night, Virginia let me see where I'd gone wrong. Instead of allowing my students to discover new thoughts, she says that I just cram ideas down their throats. It's either my way or the highway. She says I've become 'didactic and tyrannical.'" He shook his head. "When I was a student like you two, that is not the kind of teacher I wanted to be."

He rolled closer to the fireplace. "It's really too bad we can't have a fire. That would make everything perfect."

This was so unlike him. We'd gotten used to his sarcasm and his outbursts. It was hard to believe this was the same man. I wondered if being shot had provided him a different outlook on life, made him look at things in a new way.

"I guess we could ask," I said.

"No, no, that would only get you into trouble." He turned to face us. "I am going to try to change as a teacher. There were times this semester when things were going the way I'd always hoped they would. When you and I were sharing ideas. That's what my class should have been all the time." He shook his head sadly and added, "I sincerely apologize for any discomfort I've caused you."

"Thank you, sir," I said.

He nodded. "And then there's the Mormon thing. If Virginia wants to be baptized, I won't stand in her way. And I may even go to church once in a while to see what it's like." He moistened his lips with his tongue. "That's it. Any questions?"

"No. Thank you so much," Autumn said.

"I have a question," I said.

"What is it?"

"I'm wondering about our grades. With everything that's happened, do I—do we—still have a chance to get an A in your class?"

"Is that important to you?"

"Yes, sir, it is."

I explained to him how my getting an A would determine if I received a provisional acceptance to Harvard Law School. Given his mellow mood, I was hoping he might be sympathetic to me, but I was surprised. He reverted to his professorial personae.

"Whether or not you get an A is up to you," he explained. "As you once pointed out to me, you've read the syllabus. What are the three criteria?"

"Attendance is the first thing," I said, trying to remember the other two.

"And . . ." he prompted.

"Participation in class discussions," Autumn chimed in.

"And . . ." Professor Penstock said.

"Writing a term paper," I added.

"A cogent, twenty-page term paper on an approved topic," he clarified. He tapped his chin. "Well," he said. "Let's see. I don't have the roll to look at, but my recollection is that you haven't missed any classes, have you?"

"No, sir."

He smiled. "And it's been painfully evident for me that you have participated in the class discussion. Not that we've yet found anything to agree on."

"Yes, sir."

"So, it all comes down to the term paper, which, by the way, is due"—he consulted his cell phone—"on May fifth."

"Are you saying I can still earn an A?" After all we'd gone through with him, I had pretty much given up any hope.

"As I said, that depends on you—and your term paper."

I couldn't believe it. I still had a chance. I felt an impulse to shake his hand, but we weren't to that point yet.

Then his mood changed again. "Virginia said if I did a good job apologizing this morning, you might be willing to share some of that exquisite chocolate with me."

"Hey, help yourself," I blurted, passing him the open bag of chocolate on the table.

He took a piece, thanked me, and said, "I'll see you two in class," as he left the room.

From then on Dr. Penstock's class changed dramatically. He asked the students questions about what they thought. Most of the time he thanked students for offering their point of view whether he agreed with them or not. He still expressed his views, but he didn't try to tell anyone else what they should think.

He also approved a topic for my term paper: "How My Faith Sustains Me in a World of Situational Ethics."

In approving the topic, he wrote, "I probably won't agree with your conclusions, but that is no longer a requirement.

I will instead evaluate your paper based on the strength of your arguments and your skill in presenting them."

Fair enough. This was going to be the most important paper I would ever write, and I got busy immediately, assembling my thoughts and creating an outline.

Autumn was a big help as we brainstormed and I began writing. I thought it was going to be easy, but as I was defining my values, I was having trouble making it sound like a college term paper. I needed some help.

I remembered the advice I'd received from Autumn's dad and asked her if she thought her father would mind critiquing my paper. She thought that was a good idea and gave me his e-mail address. I wrote to him, asking for some help and attached the rough draft of my paper. Just a couple of hours later, he e-mailed me back with some great suggestions. One of them was to remember what President Packer had written about "staying in context" so that others will know what I believe.

That got me going, and I changed my approach to the topic, spending more effort on defining my personal values and citing examples from current events and history, showing how "situational ethics" seldom solved the problems caused by people making bad choices.

On Wednesday, April 21, Elder Bonneville returned to his home in Utah. Later that day he called Autumn. She said they talked for two hours. She got mad at me when I called him Elder Wonderful. "His name is Christopher Bonneville, and I would appreciate it if you would use his name correctly."

I told her I'd do that.

On Saturday the twenty-fourth, I baptized Mrs.

Penstock. Dr. Penstock attended the service and was cordial, if not exactly excited for her.

On Sunday, Autumn and I both attended Mrs. Penstock's ward and sat with her in sacrament meeting and Sunday School.

That was also the day Christopher spoke in his ward's sacrament meeting. His mom recorded it so Autumn could hear it. Autumn listened to it that night.

On Monday she told me she'd enjoyed his talk very much.

"I bet he had some great scriptural insights, didn't he?" I asked.

"Yes, he did, as a matter of fact."

I wondered if I'd spent less time on my mission worrying about which cars in the mission fleet needed oil changes and lube jobs and more time in the scriptures, she'd have looked up to me more.

I could see her slipping away from me. She talked a lot about Christopher. "His mom and dad have invited me to spend the summer with them. Christopher's aunt works in a bank, and she can get me a job there. It pays very well."

Hearing her talk about a future without me by her side was tearing me up, but I put on a neutral face and said, "Are you going to do that?"

"I don't know. What do you think?"

"I think it's a dumb idea. Why should you make things easy for him? If he's interested in you, make him show it. But you know what? You do whatever you think is best."

She nodded. "Yeah, I know."

"And if that doesn't work out, move to Boston, and we'll get better acquainted."

"We don't need to get better acquainted. We know each other too well as it is," she teased.

I was in no mood for her jokes. I just shook my head.

"You okay?" she asked.

"I didn't make the cut, did I?" I asked quietly.

She shook her head, "Nick, please don't do this."

"Do what?"

"Destroy what we've had."

"What we've had? And what is that? We helped each other in a class, and we worked as volunteers in the library. That's all. Oh, and we discovered we both like good chocolate. That's about it, right?"

She turned away and wouldn't look at me. "I am so sorry," she said.

"Me too," I said bitterly.

• • •

I quit going to our conference room in the library. Autumn and I still sat together in class, and we still defended our core beliefs when we needed to, but Penstock was now willing to listen to anyone's ideas. We usually spent a few minutes before class talking, but that was about it. She did tell me once that Christopher and his folks were going to fly out for her graduation.

On May fifth, we turned in our papers for Dr. Penstock's class. Because of the help I'd received from Autumn's dad as well as having Autumn proofread my paper, I thought it was the best piece of work I had done in college.

Autumn didn't need any help from me on her paper, but she did let me read it. It was exceptionally good.

When I got my paper back from Penstock, the only

marks on it were the grade—an A minus—and a handwritten note that said, "Well argued. Nice work."

No surprise that Autumn received an A for her paper.

So, after all that, I got my A in the class and the chance to go to Harvard Law School the next fall—still on a provisional basis, of course.

On Saturday, May fifteenth, Autumn and I both graduated.

After the ceremony my mom said she wanted to meet Autumn, but I thought it would have been too awkward, especially with Christopher there. I told her I'd never be able to find Autumn in that crowd.

Later, I did see Autumn, but it was at a distance. She was with her mom and dad and Elder Wonderful and his folks. I guess we could have gone over and talked to them. But I didn't tell my mom I'd seen her, and so we just made our way toward the parking lot.

I thought about taking my mom and dad to the conference room in the library but I didn't because with my luck, Autumn would be there too. Besides, that room was our room, and I didn't want to share it with anyone else.

I knew I was going to miss her terribly, but I tried not to think about it.

With Autumn and me it had always been, "Off on another adventure." But now it seemed there would be no more adventures.

Chapter Eleven

The first part of my summer was numbingly predictable, mainly because I worked for my dad in his law office. Every day I got up when he got up, ate breakfast with him, and rode to work with him. I mostly worked on tasks that not even the secretaries wanted to handle, like proofreading wills, researching case law, and attending funerals of people his firm had represented for many years. At night I worked in our family garden with my mom and dad or rode the riding lawn mower.

Autumn had given up the idea of serving in an orphanage in Ecuador because Christopher didn't want her to. Whatever Christopher wants, Christopher gets, right?

Autumn and I became Facebook friends, but I never sent her a personal message. I just sat back and watched her life unfold through her posts.

She got a job a few miles from her folks' home as a marketing director for a boutique soap company. She sent me some samples and made me promise to try them out.

They made me smell like I'd been thrown into a vat of perfume. After a couple of days though, the smell had mostly gone away.

Every morning I ran with my dad. We ran the same course and timed ourselves. He didn't like it when I ran faster than he did, so I held back.

On Sundays I served as an assistant ward clerk and helped count and record the donations for that week. I also accompanied a member of the bishopric when we made the deposit.

I read on Facebook about how Autumn spent the Fourth of July with Elder Wonderful and his family on Lake Powell. She got sunburned and had a mild case of food poisoning. The family was kind enough to look away when she hurled over the side of the boat, except, of course, for the boys in the family, who thought it was hilarious.

After that sweet, romantic interlude, she returned home.

I missed her tremendously, but, of course, I couldn't tell her that. I did send her virtual flowers once.

Sometimes early in the morning, I lay in bed and tried to decide what I lacked or what I could have done differently so that Autumn would have fallen in love with me instead of thinking of us as *just friends.*

The only thing I could think of was that my jaw didn't jut out enough. For a couple of days I tried to jut out my jaw, but after one of the secretaries at work asked me if I had a toothache, I gave it up.

As a personal improvement program, I began learning five new words a day and then using them in everyday conversation. That didn't seem to make much difference, either.

I began to read the scriptures every day, just as I had

done on my mission. I even kept a journal of scriptural insights, knowing, of course, that they would never stack up to what Christopher was churning out.

I also set a goal to do a hundred crunches a day. The first day I reached my goal, but I was so sore that it hurt to breathe deeply for three days, so I put that on hold for a while.

I finally decided that the reason Autumn apparently didn't think of me as a love interest was that we spent too much time together. Anyone can look heroic in short segments. Like in mission district meetings.

But Autumn and I had spent four to eight hours a day together for an entire semester. She'd seen me the way I am. She'd seen me blow my nose. She'd seen me spill food on my shirt. She'd seen me indecisive, bewildered, tired, and discouraged. She'd also seen me sneak chocolate from the bag when I didn't think she'd notice.

Our problem was that we worked too well together. We'd helped each other too much. We were a team. On the surface that sounds good, but picture a handsome hero coming to rescue a princess who is trapped in a prison by an evil, fire-breathing dragon. Does the hero sit down with the princess and say, "So, you got any ideas how we can get out of here? Any weaknesses in the dragon you've noticed? What hours does he keep? Let's write some things down and then decide which approach we want to take."

Does any self-respecting hero do that? I don't think so. If he did, there's no way the princess would, once they had fled the dragon, tell him "You're my hero." How can someone be your hero if you provided him with most of his good ideas?

Instead the princess would say, "Hey, it's been great

working with you. Maybe sometime, if either one of us gets captured by a dragon, we'll do this again."

And he'd say, "Absolutely. Call me."

Even though I could come up with things that might have helped Autumn love me, I knew that if I'd done those things, I'd have had less time with her. I mean I'd have been out there posturing to look heroic, and she still would have gone for Elder Wonderful.

So there I was, working in a law office, doing things I didn't enjoy, knowing the only girl I'd ever loved was out of my life. I'd basically given up on us and was spending all my time feeling sorry for myself.

One morning, though, I began to wonder if there might be some sister missionary who'd looked up to me in the same way Autumn did to Elder Wonderful. Although I'd never been a zone leader or a mission assistant, I had been in charge of the mission fleet of cars. And as luck would have it, before I'd worked in the office, I had been in a district where we had a sister companionship. Maybe one of them remembered me. I mean, anything's possible, right?

I fantasized that maybe some single, returned sister missionary spent part of every day fantasizing about me, reliving once again in her mind the zone conference when I told the missionaries to make sure they had antifreeze in their radiators. Maybe that was music to some sister missionary's ears. I mean, it shows I'm responsible and that I'm good with details, right? And what girl doesn't want that?

I picked one of the two sisters I'd served with and found her on Facebook. I was thrilled when she accepted me as a friend.

My first message to her was right to the point: "I've been thinking about you lately."

She sent me an ice-cold drink. Of course it was only a virtual ice-cold drink, but still it was something, you know what I mean? We were interacting on a virtual ice-cold drink basis. Who knows where something like that can lead?

So I called her. "Hi, I bet you can't guess who this is, can you?"

"Elder Baxter?"

"Yes, that's right! Good job! How did you guess?"

"Your voice. It's unmistakable."

"Really? In what way?"

A long pause. "Actually, I'd rather not say."

Ouch. "Well, no matter. How are you doing?"

"Okay, I guess. Why are you calling me?" she asked.

"Do you ever think about me late at night or early in the morning?"

"Why would I do that?" she shot back.

"Well, you remember that time on your mission when you complained about the smell in your car, and I found a decomposing squirrel in your wheel well? As I remember, you were totally grateful to me for finding it. Good times, right?"

Long pause. "Actually, you know what? I have to go."

This was not going as well as I would have liked.

"Sure, I understand. When would be a good time to call you again?"

She hung up on me.

I wasn't discouraged until a few hours later when she totally dropped me as a Facebook friend without even as much as another virtual ice-cold drink.

But I wasn't completely discouraged. There were other sisters who'd needed my help with their mission cars. Five, to be exact.

Over the next few days, I found out that three were married, one was engaged, and the other had already hung up on me.

I admit, after that, I might have been just a little discouraged.

But then I realized the answer had been right under my nose all the time. A girl in my stake was working as an intern in my dad's office. She was also efficient, so we had a lot in common.

I approached her during lunch. She was eating a sprout-and-avocado wrap and drinking distilled water that she brought from home every day.

"You want to go out sometime?" I asked.

"With you?"

"Yes."

"I'm only eighteen. How old are you?"

"Uh, twenty-two."

She shook her head. "I don't think so."

"Look, we could just go to the movies. That way you wouldn't even have to talk to me."

"You look a lot like your dad, and he's lost all his hair."

That made me mad. "I have plenty of hair, okay? You don't need to worry about my hair status. Look, is it going to kill you to go to a stupid movie with me?"

Apparently she'd been working in a lawyer's office too long. "Do you think that what you're doing now might possibly fall into the category of inappropriate workplace harassment? I mean, your dad is my boss, and you're asking me out. You want me to connect the dots for you?"

"Look, just forget it, okay?"

"No problem there," she said, taking another bite of her precious sandwich.

So, bottom line, I gave up on her.

Eventually I decided that there would probably be lots of eligible LDS girls at Harvard. They'd probably respect any guy going to law school, especially if they were freshman girls. *Oh, yeah,* I thought, *it's going to be a whole new ball game once I get to Harvard.*

But in the meantime I joined an LDS online dating service. Trying to paint the best picture of me, I did ten revisions on the questions they asked about me. I also went to a professional photographer to get just the right picture. And then, even after that, I ended up having to Photoshop it to get it the way I wanted.

Six girls expressed an interest in getting to know me better. One lived in Alaska, one in Russia, one in South Africa, one in Denmark, one in North Dakota, and one in Fishtail, Montana.

Things were going well with the four who understood English, but not so much with the girls from Russia and Denmark. The girl from Russia was so stunningly beautiful that I promised her I would learn Russian even though I didn't think I really could. Finally it occurred to me that quite possibly I was a pathetic loser, running after an impossible dream, stupidly hoping some magical, random spark would flare up into a serious relationship.

Things were so bad I started to watch *Scooby-Doo* episodes. Sometimes at work, when I was feeling good, I'd say out loud what the bad guy always says at the end of the show: "And we'd have done it, too, if it weren't for those meddlesome kids." Some people in the office ended up feeling sorry for my dad.

On the second Monday in July, mid-morning, I got a surprise phone call.

"Hi, Nick, it's Autumn." She spoke in her little girl voice—the one she used whenever she was disappointed or sad or discouraged.

"What's wrong?" I asked.

"My dad had a stroke two days ago. It wasn't major, and the doctor thinks he's going to mostly recover. But I knew you'd want to know."

I felt awful. Her dad was a great guy, and he had helped me a lot, especially with my term paper. "So he's going to be okay, right?" I asked.

"We sure hope so. He's out of the hospital and back home, so that's good."

We talked for over an hour. She was having a hard time dealing with things. Her dad had always been her rock and seeing him incapacitated, even a little, had shaken her.

Finally I asked, "What can I do to help out?"

"Nothing; we're good."

"What's your biggest concern?"

"My dad keeps wanting to get up and go to work, but there's no way he can do it. His speech is slurred, and he has a hard time walking. He knows what needs to be done in the office, but he has a hard time communicating it. This is an election year, and one of the members of the city council will be running against him. His name is William Corvallis, and he says my dad should step down, which would automatically put Corvallis in as acting mayor without an election. The guy is a snake, and he and Dad have been at odds from day one. Dad doesn't want him to be the next mayor because of all the damage he'd do."

"Sounds complicated."

"Yeah, it is. I don't know what to do. My mom is a wreck. I'm trying to help out at home, but I'm also trying to keep up on city business for my dad. The thing is, there's just not enough of me."

I hated hearing how discouraged and worried she was. "What if I came out there for a few days to help out?"

No answer. "Autumn, you still there?"

"Would you actually do that for us?" she asked softly.

"Yeah, sure. I'm just working for my dad. I'm sure he'll understand."

"I can't believe you'd do that."

"Tell you what, I'll leave right after I tell my dad and go home to pack a few things."

I was wrong about my dad being understanding. "You act like what we do here is of no importance," he complained after I explained what I was going to do.

"I know it's important, Dad, but not as important as helping out a friend."

"How long will this take?"

"I don't know. Just a few days."

"You're not asking permission, are you? You're telling me what you're going to do. What if I weren't your father? What if I were your employer? Would you just run off from a job like this?"

"I actually think I would. Sorry."

"I'm not sure what you'll ever contribute to society with an attitude like that."

"You're probably right, Dad." I forced a smile and retrieved my keys from my pocket. "Well, you take care, okay? I'm going home to get packed. I'll call when I get to Autumn's house so you'll know I had a safe trip."

"Your mom would appreciate that."

"Yeah, I know *she* would." The implication, of course, was that he wouldn't.

So I went home, packed, and left. My mom didn't say much except to ask me what my dad had said. I told her. She didn't seem surprised.

Just before I got in my car to leave, she gave me a big hug and told me she loved me and was proud of me for wanting to help out Autumn's family.

Three hours later when I pulled into Autumn's driveway, she came running out to see me. As soon as I got out of the car, she threw her arms around me. She started crying, so we just held on to each other for a long time.

Eventually, she pulled away, wiped her tears, and sighed. "You'll never know what it means to me that you came here."

"Hey, what are friends for, right? How's your dad doing?"

"Better today. You want to see him?"

"Sure, if he's up to it."

We found her mom in the bedroom feeding him applesauce. About half of every spoonful dribbled down his chin.

Her mom got up and gave me a hug. "Thank you so much for coming."

"I want to help out any way I can."

"I know. We're very grateful."

She turned to her husband. "Daryl, look who's here!"

He smiled faintly. I wasn't certain he even knew who I was.

Autumn wiped some applesauce from his chin. "It's Nick, Daddy. My friend from college."

He said something I didn't understand.

"He's going to be here for a few days to help out. Isn't that great?" Autumn asked.

He nodded.

We stayed for a few more minutes while they filled me in on Daryl's condition. Basically, he'd get better in time. How much better, nobody knew.

Autumn took me into the kitchen and warmed some casserole that the Relief Society had brought over. "While you're here, we need you to eat all the food people have brought us. We can't keep up with it."

"I can help with that," I said with a smile.

She smiled. "I know you can."

Her mom told me I could stay in the same room where I'd stayed before. She took me to the bathroom, pointed out clean towels for me on the towel rack, and told me to put my dirty clothes in the hamper so she could wash them for me.

We ate first, and then I mowed their lawn, did some weeding, and brought in some fresh produce from their garden.

"What else can I do?" I asked Autumn.

"After dinner can we go to my dad's office? There are a lot of issues that are piling up, and some people are demanding my dad resign as mayor, but I know he wouldn't want to do that, especially if he's going to get better. We need to work through those issues for him."

It was about seven that night when we arrived at the city office building. There was nobody else there. We ended up in the conference room, the one with the whiteboard and the long table.

Autumn's dad was obviously not able to function as mayor, and I wasn't sure we had the authority to really do anything without his consent. But we worked until eleven that night, doing our best. By the time we finished, we had worked up a priorities list of what needed to be done in the next few days. At first we generated it on the whiteboard and then continued to revise it until we were in total agreement, and then we wrote it all down in a notebook.

"I feel good about what we accomplished tonight," Autumn said as we drove home.

"Yeah, me too. So, Autumn and Nick are off for another adventure, right?"

She smiled. "Yeah, just like in *Scooby-Doo*."

After a few moments of silence, I asked, "So . . . how's Christopher?"

"Good." No comment for several seconds. "He sent me a copy of his patriarchal blessing."

"Why would he do that?"

"I'm not sure. I guess he's proud of it." She sighed. "Also, he asked me to send him a copy of my patriarchal blessing."

"I don't think you're supposed to do that—share your blessing with someone who's not a member of your family. You're not going to do that, are you?"

She hesitated.

"Don't. It's none of his business . . . unless you're engaged. You're not engaged, are you?"

"No, of course not."

"Tell him no then. Did he ask you for it so he wouldn't have to go to a lot of effort to get to know you better? Or is he shopping for the girl with the most impressive eternal potential?"

"I don't know."

"This is so wrong. I have no respect for him."

"He just wants to do what Heavenly Father wants him to do."

"Well, let me make that simple for him then! Heavenly Father wants him to spend time with a girl, fall in love with her, and then decide if he wants to marry her. There's no shortcut to that process."

She lowered her head and didn't say anything for a long time. "Actually, I've already sent him a copy of my patriarchal blessing."

I sighed. "Oh. Never mind then." I opened her car door, and we headed toward her front door.

"He must have received it by now, but he hasn't contacted me about it."

"Are you worried he might think you're not noble enough?"

"I don't know. Maybe."

"What has he said about your dad?"

"He said he was sorry to hear it."

"And did he do that on Facebook?"

That made her mad. "No! Why do you hate him so much? We talk every day for a few minutes. He's very busy."

"Sorry."

At the door she stopped me. "Could you just hold me for a while?"

"Okay."

"But not kiss me."

"I know."

And so I held her in my arms. And she started crying. I just kept saying, "Everything's going to be okay." I must have said it five or six times.

Finally, she kissed me on the cheek, thanked me, and we both went inside to our separate rooms.

The next morning, I told Autumn that it felt awkward staying in her house, even though I had my own room. For one thing we were sharing a bathroom, which added to my discomfort. It looked as though I might be staying longer than I had originally thought. Nothing inappropriate was going to happen between us, of course, but I was still uneasy about the living arrangements.

"Maybe you're right," she said.

Without a job I didn't have the money to go to a hotel, and I didn't know how to solve the problem. But while we were eating breakfast, Autumn had a thought.

"Why don't I call the bishop? Maybe he knows of someplace in the ward where you could stay."

That turned out to be the answer. There was a couple in the ward whose two sons weren't living at home—one of them was on a mission, and the other had just gotten married and moved out. Brother and Sister Falcone generously agreed to let me sleep at their house for as long as I needed. I packed up and moved over there that very afternoon, which took a lot of pressure off Autumn and me.

• • •

A day or two later, William J. Corvallis, senior member of the city council, was featured on the front page of the local newspaper stating that he had been informed by someone on the hospital staff that Autumn's father was not going to recover sufficiently to continue as mayor. Corvallis demanded that the city council appoint a new interim mayor until November when the regularly scheduled election would be held.

"Would you be willing to serve as the interim mayor?" the reporter had asked.

"If that's what the city council wants. I am always willing to serve my community. And, in fact, I have just this morning placed my name on the ballot for mayor for the November election."

As soon as Autumn and I had finished some chores around the house, we went to the city council conference room and made full use of the whiteboard again.

We ended up with two immediate objectives. First, to establish that her dad, although somewhat limited, was still functioning as mayor. And, second, to show that he would, in time, recover fully.

The most important issue at the next city council meeting would be Corvallis's motion to repeal a law that prohibited large chain stores from existing in the town. The ordinance had been passed ten years earlier, and now Walmart was proposing building a superstore within the city limits.

It took us over an hour to explain this to Autumn's dad. Once he understood, he shook his head and slurred, "No Walmart."

We attended the regularly scheduled city council meeting

that week. Corvallis, as senior member of the city council, conducted. His first item of business was to move that an interim mayor be named by the city council.

At that point, Autumn and I stood up and asked to present a progress report on the mayor's condition.

Corvallis glared at us. "This meeting is not yet open to public comments."

"I'm the mayor's daughter."

"I know who you are. Please sit down so the council can proceed with its official business."

A member of the city council objected. "I want to hear how Daryl is doing. Let her tell us."

Corvallis sighed loudly.

"Oh, get off your high horse, Bill, and let the girl speak!" another city councilman complained.

Corvallis frowned and then made a gesture for Autumn to come to the front of the room.

Members of the city council sat behind two long tables, with Corvallis in the middle. A small lectern was set on the table in front of him.

Autumn stood facing the city council. "Thank you for giving me this time. I would also like to thank Nicolas Baxter, my associate, a student at Harvard Law School, who has agreed to assist me during my dad's recovery time."

Before beginning her presentation, she took time to look at each member of the council, including Corvallis, who was not happy at the intrusion on his path to victory.

"I am happy to report that my dad is doing a little better every day. Nicolas and I talked to him at some length in preparation for this meeting. He gave us direction about the business that would be considered tonight, and we will be happy to report on his wishes as the meeting continues."

"Is he walking?" Corvallis asked.

"No, not yet."

"Is he feeding himself?"

"No."

"And what about bathroom usage? I assume you have him in a diaper, right?"

Autumn scowled. "Excuse me. Are you a doctor?"

He shook his head. "Are you an elected member of the city council?" He lifted his hands in exasperation. "I object to your taking valuable time from our very full agenda."

She ignored the comment. "I want to report that the mayor is still in opposition to any ruling that would make it possible for big-box stores to be permitted in this community."

"And how did he express that opinion?" Corvallis asked. "With a nod of his head? With a mumble? If so, how do you know he even understood the question?"

I came and stood next to Autumn. "As someone who is not a member of the family, I can report that the mayor fully understood the question, and, in fact, said, 'No Walmart.'"

Corvallis glared at me. "And why, if I may ask, are you here at this meeting? Have you been hired to represent the mayor?"

"No."

"What year did you say you were in law school?"

"I will be in my first year in the fall."

He smirked. "So, in other words, you haven't even taken one law class at Harvard. Is that correct?"

"Yes, but I am working in my dad's law office this summer."

"So what brought you to town?"

"Autumn asked me."

"How does she even know you?"

"We worked together on several projects as volunteers in the Gresham University Library this past year. We work very well together," I said.

"Yes, I'm sure you do," Corvallis joked. Nobody laughed.

"I take offense at that remark," Autumn said.

"I apologize for it then. But I do not apologize for my position that stores like Walmart will bring jobs to this community. And we desperately need jobs."

"At what expense?" Autumn asked. "It will cause many of our local stores to go out of business."

"If they can't compete, maybe they should close."

A member of the city council raised his hand and was recognized by Corvallis. "I think we should wait until the mayor returns before we make a decision on this matter."

"And how long will we wait?" Corvallis asked. "Six months? A year? Walmart is not going to wait that long. If we don't jump on this now, they'll build a new store in Garden Grove, and we'll lose our business to another town. Is that what we want? We need to act now."

"Let's give the mayor some time to recuperate," another member of the city council said.

"All right then," Corvallis grumbled. "How about two weeks? That ought to be long enough. Let him come here himself and discuss his reasons for opposing progress in this community. And if he can't, then I insist we appoint an interim mayor."

"That is acceptable to me," the city councilman said. The others agreed.

Autumn and I looked at each other. Neither one of us thought two weeks would be enough time.

But that's all we had to work with.

Chapter Twelve

Once Christopher learned I was spending every day with Autumn, he began phoning her every night around eleven o'clock our time. The only thing she'd tell me about what they said was that he'd been impressed with her patriarchal blessing.

I thought any guy who'd decide to marry a girl just because of her patriarchal blessing was not someone you could trust. But I kept that opinion to myself—mostly.

"Would you like to read my patriarchal blessing?" she asked one day.

"No, I would not," I said. "That's between you and Father in Heaven."

"Oh." She paused. "You don't think it was a good idea for me to send it to Christopher, do you?"

"I've already told you that."

"Anything else you'd like to tell me?"

"Don't agree to marry him when you're so far away from each other. You've never gone out with him. You've never seen him in jeans and a sweatshirt. You don't know if he has a temper. You don't know how he treats his mom when you're not around."

"You don't like him at all, do you?"

"I can't say if I do or not. You know why? Because I've never spent any time with him. Just like you, right?"

"He wants me to move to Utah and work for his aunt in the fall. She's an executive at a bank. It would be a very good job, and it pays well."

I'd had it with her. "That's what you should do then," I said.

"Why do you say that?" she asked.

"If you were in Utah, you'd see each other all the time, and that would make any decision you make about him more rational."

"I see your point." She paused. "I'm sorry for . . ." Her voice trailed off.

I tried to sound upbeat. "There's nothing to be sorry about. I've always known we were just friends."

"Yeah, best friends for sure. And now we're off on other adventures, right?" She sighed. "Although, maybe not together."

I figured that was her way of telling me there was no possibility of us ever having a serious relationship.

Oh, well, I thought, *things will pick up once I'm at Harvard.* Every mom wants her daughter to marry either a doctor or a lawyer, so I hoped that would give me an advantage.

• • •

For the next two weeks, we did all we could to make it possible for Autumn's dad to conduct business at the next city council meeting.

We didn't trust him to walk into the meeting because he was still a little shaky. Against his objections, we got him to agree that he'd enter the room in a wheelchair but would conduct the meeting standing up, using the rostrum to help him maintain his balance.

One big problem was that he slurred his words when he spoke. We cut out articles from the local paper and had him read them as if he were speaking to the city council. We practiced fifteen minutes in the morning and fifteen minutes in the afternoon. Sometimes at night we'd hear him practicing in their bedroom.

I wanted him to work out a strategy for the meeting with two good friends who also served on the city council, but Autumn told me that would be interpreted as a private meeting and would be illegal.

We made up three-by-five cards summarizing issues that had been discussed by the city council over the past year. We read these to Daryl over and over so if he was asked a question, he'd be able to show that his mind was working well.

On the day of the meeting, we felt like we'd prepared him for any issue that might be brought up. We just wanted him to look competent enough to continue serving as mayor.

Everything went well at the city council meeting for the first forty-five minutes. The city council delayed making a decision about letting Walmart build in the town; the only one who objected was William J. Corvallis.

The meeting was almost over when Corvallis stood up. "There is one issue that I would like to discuss, and that is the failure of the city to responsibly manage its funds. Mayor, perhaps you can explain this." He held up a copy of a cancelled check. "I found this in your desk. It appears to be a city account, but, if so, it's from an account we've never heard of. I found several cancelled checks, all with just one signature, in violation of City Statute 3.12. Furthermore, the cancelled checks do not seem to be for city business. And so I was wondering, Mayor, can you explain to the council the existence of a secret account which bypasses accepted accounting procedures?"

Autumn's dad seemed confused.

It didn't look good. I stood up. "I can assure you that we will look into this and make a complete report at the next meeting."

"Tell us again who you are," Corvallis said. "For the benefit of the newspaper reporter at our meeting tonight."

"I am an associate of the mayor."

"And who pays your salary?"

"I'm serving as an intern . . . without pay."

"And on what day was this intern position approved of by the city council?" Corvallis asked.

"It wasn't. I just came when I heard about the mayor's condition."

"So, in reality, you have no official standing with this council or with the mayor, do you?"

"No, but—"

Corvallis interrupted me. "Because of the mayor's utter disregard for city policies, and also because of the possibility of misuse of city funds, I demand the mayor resign immediately."

"And who would then be the acting mayor?" I asked.

"Well, I suppose I would, since I am senior member of the city council."

"How convenient for you," I said. "No, the mayor will

not resign. Furthermore, we will answer your questions as soon as we can."

"And how long would you like for that?"

"Maybe a week."

"A week? You can't be serious! We're talking about misuse of city funds here! Listen to me, you have two days! That's all! I'm not going to let you drag this out forever."

I nodded. "We'll be ready in two days then."

"I will be very interested in what you come up with. Very interested, indeed."

I leaned over to Autumn's dad. "How do we end this thing?"

He seemed stumped.

Autumn stepped to his side. "Dad, I think all you have to do is declare the meeting adjourned."

He did, and it was over.

After the meeting Corvallis asked to speak to me privately. He led me into an office and closed the door. "I want you to see this," he said, showing me a cancelled check for three hundred dollars made out to a Susanna Stansbury.

"For your information," he said, "Susanna Stansbury is a twenty-eight-year-old dancer. So naturally I'm interested in knowing why some exotic dancer received three hundred dollars from the mayor. Is she a friend of his, and if so, how good a friend?"

"I don't know. But I'll find out."

He put his hand on my shoulder in an imitation of a fatherly gesture. "Look, I don't want to hurt the mayor's reputation, so if you'll talk him and the family into agreeing to announce his retirement when the city council meets in two days, I'll keep my mouth shut, give you the cancelled checks, and you'll never hear from me again about this matter."

My first instinct was to punch him out, but I didn't. Why? Because I knew how devastated Autumn would be if it became public knowledge that her dad had been seeing another woman and had misused city funds, if either of those things had actually happened. And so, because of that, I decided it might be best to keep my options open.

After a long pause, I nodded and said, "Let me see what I can do."

"Very good. I think him resigning would be for the best."

"Can I have the cancelled check?" I asked.

"You can have a copy of it," he said, reaching into his binder and handing it to me. And then he left.

On the back of the cancelled check, Susanna Stansbury had signed her name and written, "Thanks! You're the best!"

I felt sick to my stomach.

A reporter from the local paper approached me and asked about the mayor's secret fund.

"You'll be the first to know once we find out what's going on," I said. I had him give me his number.

Although Autumn and I assured her dad that he had done well, we both knew he'd be in serious trouble unless we could come up with a legitimate explanation for what would most certainly end up being called the mayor's slush fund.

We took her dad home and talked briefly to her mom about the city council meeting, but didn't say anything about the secret checking account.

I asked Autumn to take a walk with me. We headed

for the playground at the grade school she'd attended. We sat next to each other on the swing set and I told her what Corvallis had told me about Susanna Stansbury.

When I finished, she turned away and wouldn't talk, but I could hear her crying.

"You okay?" I asked after several minutes.

She shook her head. "This is too much. I can't handle it."

"I know."

"What is my mom going to do if she finds out my dad has been having an affair?"

"We don't know that. It's probably all a big mistake. I'm sure he's completely innocent. We just have to talk to this Susanna, that's all."

While we were still at the school, I called Susanna Stansbury, told her I worked for the mayor, and asked if we could come by. She said she would be glad to see us the next afternoon, and we made an appointment with her. I also asked her that if anyone else came by to talk to her, to refuse to say anything until we had a chance to meet with her. She said that wouldn't be a problem.

On our way back home, Autumn said, "I'm never going to be able to get any sleep tonight. Can you stay up with me? We could watch movies."

"Yeah, sure, whatever you want."

She sighed. "You're so good to me."

"Hey, we're a team."

"Yeah, we are."

In the TV room, we selected some movies to watch. And then we sat on the couch, her snuggling up to me, and turned on the first one.

At two in the morning, I woke up. She'd been sleeping too.

I touched her shoulder. "Autumn, it's late. Let's just go to bed."

She looked confused.

"I mean in different houses," I added.

She nodded, stood up, walked like a zombie to her room, and shut the door.

I drove to where I was staying and soon fell back to sleep.

The next afternoon, on our way to Susanna's house, Autumn told me she was preparing herself for the worst. "This looks really bad. I don't know if I'm up to hearing what this is all about. I mean . . . what if . . . ?"

"Let's just wait until we've talked to her," I cautioned.

"I feel like I'm going to be sick," she said.

"Not in my car, okay?"

She gave me a thin little smile.

Susanna lived in a modest house. After we knocked, Susanna came to the door wearing a black leotard. She was a beautiful woman.

I introduced myself.

"Hi. Give me five minutes. I'm just finishing up a class. Come into my studio in back."

Autumn avoided looking at Susanna as we followed her to the studio. The girls in the dance class looked to be about fourteen years old, and they kept looking over at us, so when they were done, we stood and clapped. "Very nice work, girls!" I called out.

They seemed pleased as they filed out of the studio.

After all the girls were gone, Susanna joined us at the

back of the studio. She put on a robe over her dance outfit and pulled up a chair in front of us.

"What can I do for you?" she asked, smiling.

I said to her, "Thanks for seeing us. You may not be aware of it, but Mayor Jones has had a minor stroke and is still recovering. We're helping him tie up a few loose ends, and we have a question about something we think you can help us with. Last year the mayor wrote you a check for three hundred dollars. We need to know what it was for."

She smiled. "The mayor has been so good to me!"

Autumn winced.

"In what way?" I asked.

"Well, the girls you saw just now were selected to appear at a national competition in Las Vegas. I went to the mayor to see if there were any city funds that could at least pay for gas and some lodging for the girls. He said he was proud of us, and he sat down and wrote out a check for three hundred dollars."

"And how did the team do?" I asked.

"Out of twenty-five teams, we made the top five."

"Congratulations," Autumn said, suddenly back to her old self. "By the way, I'm Autumn. I'm the mayor's daughter."

"You tell your dad he's one of my heroes."

"I will. Thank you."

Autumn was relieved, but I was still worried her dad had used city funds without authorization from the city council.

On our drive home, it occurred to me that we had been so consumed by our concerns, we hadn't done anything to have any fun together.

"You want to go do something? Maybe get something to eat?" I asked.

She looked at me. "Have you got any money?"

"Uh, nope. . . . have you?"

"Uh-uh," she confessed.

"I've got a credit card," I offered. When she didn't immediately take my offer, I added an additional enticement, "KFC? What do you say?"

She looked over at me and grinned. "It's not often that a girl gets invited to have dinner with the Colonel. How can I refuse?"

I had offered KFC, but at the last minute decided to take Autumn to a nice, sit-down restaurant. The hostess sat us in a booth at the rear of the dining room where we were pretty much alone while we ate.

As the waitress was clearing our table, she asked if we had left room for dessert.

I grinned. "Let's get a pie," I suggested.

"You mean a piece of pie?" Autumn asked.

"No, baby! I'm talkin' a whole pie!"

"To take home?" Autumn said.

"No, to eat right here," I clarified.

"You're kidding," she said.

"Watch and learn," I said and turned to the waitress. "Do you have coconut cream pie?"

"Sure."

"Then bring us one. You don't need to put it in a box. But we will need another couple of forks."

She gave me a funny look but went to get the pie.

"What are you going to do?" Autumn asked.

"Eat some pie! And you are too!"

The waitress set down the pie between us, and I handed Autumn a fork. Then I started in on it. Autumn stared at me in amazement. I looked up at her and with my mouth full of pie, said, "Dig in!"

She did, tentatively at first, and then it became a game to see who could eat the most. We laughed hysterically while dueling with our forks for the biggest bite. Our astonished waitress went into the kitchen and brought out two of the cooks to watch us from a distance.

After we had eaten about half of the pie and the rest had spilled all over the table, we each took a big breath, sat back, and looked at each other.

"Oh," Autumn moaned. "I think I'm going to be sick."

She had some of the pie crust in her hair, which I graciously picked out.

She returned the favor by reaching over with her napkin and wiping some cream off my face.

"We're like two monkeys at the zoo grooming each other," I said.

"What is it about you and monkeys?" she teased.

We went to pay our bill, and the manager said with a laugh, "Wow, I've never seen that before. Don't worry about the check. It's on me."

We laughed all the way home, but as we pulled into her driveway, Autumn said, "Let's sit here in the car for a few minutes."

"Okay."

It had gotten dark, and she sat for a moment without saying anything while I waited. Then she said, "Driving over to Susanna's house today, not knowing why my dad had given money to her—that was very difficult for me."

"I know."

"But then, a thought came to me, and it was, 'No matter how this turns out, Nick will help me get through it.' And that's true, isn't it? You'd have helped me, just like you're helping my family now."

"Yeah, I would. We'd have gotten through it."

She was sitting in the passenger seat with her hands folded in her lap and was staring straight ahead. The only light was coming from the porch light, and in the near-darkness, I looked at her face and realized once again how much I cared for her—how hard it was to be just her friend.

I asked her, "Why are you thinking of moving to Utah to be with Christopher?"

She shook her head. "Good question. I don't know. I'm a little confused right now. I don't know what I want."

I was about to tell her I loved her when she spoke first and asked me for a priesthood blessing.

"To help you decide whether to go to Utah?" I asked.

"Partly, but also, because it's so hard to see my dad like this."

"I can do that. When?"

"Maybe Sunday after church."

"Okay."

"I'll probably be fasting, but you don't need to," she said.

"I'll fast too."

"Thank you. Normally I'd ask my dad, but . . ." She sighed.

"I know. I'm happy to do whatever I can to help. Ask your mom if she'd like a blessing too."

"I will. Thank you so much. You're the best."

We got out of the car and went inside. Autumn's mom

was tending to her husband. When she was finished, she came into the kitchen where we talked briefly about what had happened at the city council meeting, doing our best not to alarm her.

A short time later her mom went to bed.

"Stay a little longer," Autumn said. "Let's watch *Scooby-Doo*."

I groaned. "Again? Why?"

"Because that's who we are."

"You mean immature?"

"You got it. C'mon, I'll make us some nachos," she offered.

The last thing either of us wanted was more food, and I groaned in mock pain. I did end up staying, even though I had a hard time staying awake. It had been a great evening, but I was glad when it was over and I could finally go to the Falcones' house and go to bed.

• • •

The next morning Autumn and I met with the city accountant. He didn't know anything about the account or its origin, and that was bad because it meant it had never been audited.

"If these *are* city funds, your dad is in trouble," I said.

We looked in her dad's desk drawer. We didn't find the stack of cancelled checks Corvallis had mentioned. I assumed he'd taken those for evidence. But in a file folder under a stack of similar folders in the bottom drawer of his desk, we found bank statements for the account. Every month there had been a deposit of fifty dollars. The question was, what was the source of that money?

We went back to the house and looked at her dad's personal checking account. For the past five years the mayor had deposited fifty dollars into the city account. We asked Autumn's dad why he'd set up the account. He had regained much of his ability to speak, and he explained: "Too much red tape. People come in all the time and want the city to help with their programs. There's no way the city can do that. So I donated part of my paycheck every month into a fund that I could control without having to go to anyone for approval. That's why."

We called several of the people who had received a check from the mayor's fund. Each of them confirmed that the mayor had generously responded to a special need. We asked them all to come to the city council meeting the next day and be prepared to explain what had happened.

The last thing I did was phone Corvallis and thank him for giving us more time. I told him the mayor had no intention to resign. He told me we were making a big mistake. I told him I had to go and hung up.

I also phoned the reporter who'd been at the last city council meeting and summarized briefly what I would be presenting that night.

At the city council meeting, I explained what Autumn and I had learned about the checking account, and then added, "We've taken the liberty of asking some of the recipients of these funds to tell us what the money was used for."

Susanna was first. She told of the mayor's assistance in getting her dance team to the Las Vegas competition.

A Little League baseball coach was next. "If it weren't for the mayor's help, our baseball team never would have had the travel funds we needed to compete for the regional title after we won the district tournament."

Four others gave reports. The last person said, "I think we should let the mayor know how grateful we are for his generosity." He began clapping and everyone in the room joined in—everyone, that is, except for William J. Corvallis.

After it quieted down, Corvallis said, "As well-intentioned as this may have been, it still constitutes an improper use of city funds."

"These are not city funds," I said. "The mayor has been depositing fifty dollars a month of his own money into this account."

"Once they were deposited into a city account, they became city funds," Corvallis shot back.

"These funds were never deposited into a city account," I said.

"Look at this check. It clearly indicates it's from the city," Corvallis argued.

"This was an account set up by the mayor. It was his account. Instead of having his name on the check, he chose to make it look as if it had come from the city."

"Why would he do that?" Corvallis asked.

"So the people who received the money would be grateful to the city, and not to him personally."

"It's still a criminal activity," Corvallis argued. "Falsely representing city funds."

I laughed. "You made that up, didn't you? Nice try. How can any of this be illegal if it's his money?" I addressed the other members on the council. "This is the way it looks to me: What Mayor Jones lacks in accountant know-how is more than made up for by his love for this city and its people."

Friends of the mayor agreed and made quite a commotion until Corvallis gaveled the room to silence and adjourned the meeting.

But I knew it wasn't over.

Chapter Thirteen

On Sunday after church I gave both Autumn and her mom a priesthood blessing. Because I'd been fasting and because I'd pleaded with Father in Heaven for help, I was able to give Autumn a blessing that was not compromised by my feelings for her. Even so, the blessing didn't give her any clear direction for what she should do about Christopher's invitation to move to Utah.

After I finished, and while we waited for lunch to be ready, she asked if she could talk to me in the backyard.

We sat on the porch steps, still in our Sunday clothes.

"This is awkward," she said, "but I don't know who else to talk to. You're my best friend. I trust that you always have my best interests in mind."

I knew where this was going.

She continued. "First of all, I've decided I'm going to stay here and help my dad until the election is over."

"I'll do that too, then."

"You can't, Nick. The election isn't until November, and you'll be in law school fall semester."

"No problem. I'll just start winter term—or spring term, if I have to."

"Are you sure they'll let you do that?" she asked.

"Oh, yeah, people do it all the time." Even as I said it, I doubted it was true. I suspected that when a first-year student didn't show up, Harvard gave the slot to someone else.

"Will you help me brainstorm about going to Utah after the election?" she asked.

We went inside, grabbed a piece of paper and a pencil and sat down at the dining room table. I made two columns: *Reasons to go to Utah* and *Reasons not to go*.

"If you don't go to Utah, what will you do?" I asked.

"I guess I'll see if can still work in an orphanage in Ecuador for six months."

"Are you in love with Christopher?"

"No, not really. I respect him though."

"If you don't love him, then why go out there to live?"

She thought about it for a long time and then said, "You're right. There's no reason to go."

I felt a surge of happiness that I'd won, or at least that I hadn't lost to Christopher. But then I looked down at the sheet of paper and its two columns. Whenever we'd done an exercise like this before, we tried to consider every possibility. And, in this case, we hadn't.

I wanted to keep my mouth shut, but I couldn't. "Unless . . ."

"Unless what?"

"Unless you're worried that if you don't go, you might

spend the rest of your life wondering how things would have turned out if you'd gone to see him."

She nodded. "That has occurred to me."

I sighed. "Then maybe you should go."

She sighed. "Maybe so."

Just then her mom opened the back door and told us that lunch was ready.

What have I done? I thought as I followed Autumn into the house.

• • •

A few days later I drove home and told my dad I wasn't going to start at Harvard in the fall. He was so angry with me that he stormed out and wouldn't talk to me when he came back.

My mom assured me he'd be fine once he cooled down.

I didn't want to stay at home feeling like such a disappointment to my dad, so after having a good talk with my mom, I gave her a hug and drove back to Scottsburg.

The next week my dad wrote me a letter on official stationery from his law office. He informed me that I should not expect him to intercede with the dean of the Harvard Law School again, and that whatever I did, I would have to do it on my own. He also said that he would not support me financially in law school or in any graduate program. His closing words were, "If you want to be treated as an adult, then you will have to learn to accept the consequences of bad choices." He signed it, "Love, Dad."

I realized then that if I ever did get a law degree, I would not be working in my dad's law office. Strangely enough, that didn't bother me much.

I made the mistake of showing my dad's letter to Autumn. She read it and said, "So? Most people I know don't expect their folks to pay their way through graduate school."

"You're taking his side?" I complained.

"It's his money. He doesn't owe you a thing."

"Then why didn't he just call and tell me that?" I asked. "Why does he have to send it on office stationery? Does he think this whole thing is a business relationship?"

"Look, don't let this build up a barrier between you and your dad. Call him, talk to him, let him know you understand, let him know you still love him. He's your dad. He still loves you."

I shook my head. "He's got a strange way of showing it."

She was getting mad at me. "You're always so full of advice for me about my life, but one of the few times I give you advice, you just trash it? I expected more from you."

"Everyone expects more of me. In that way, you're just like my dad."

"You know what? I give up," she said as she stormed away.

We treated each other coolly for a day or two, but because we had to work so closely together for her dad's campaign, I eventually went to her and apologized for my egregious behavior.

Her eyebrows shot up when I used the word *egregious,* and then she smiled, and I did too. We talked until things were good again between us.

The next day she challenged me to spell *egregious.* I spelled it wrong on purpose so she'd have something to tease me about.

Autumn never did tell me what her decision was about going to Utah and working for Christopher's aunt. I don't think it was secrecy; I think it was just because we were both so busy.

• • •

William J. Corvallis waged an aggressive campaign for mayor, every few days accusing Autumn's father of misconduct in office. It was all we could do to deal with the false information and rumors he spread.

From then until election day in November, Autumn and I worked as hard as we could to get her dad re-elected. Every morning we had a planning meeting in the city conference room, using the whiteboard to prioritize what we'd do that day.

Every Saturday we walked the streets visiting every house and giving out the campaign materials we had designed.

Almost weekly, William J. Corvallis leveled yet another false charge against the mayor. We were constantly having to set the record straight.

On November 2, the day of the election, there was nothing else we could do except wait for the results. We wrote up two statements, one for if her dad won and another for if he lost.

By midafternoon we were both so wired we decided to take a walk through one of the city's nature parks. Even though it was November, it was a beautiful, sunny day with little wind. There were still red and yellow leaves on the trees, but they weren't going to be there much longer.

"Whatever happens, I want you to know how much my family and I appreciate all you've done for us," Autumn said.

"It was a good experience. I learned a lot."

"Me too." She pursed her lips. "Next week I will be moving to Utah."

This was news to me. After a long awkward pause, I said, "I hope that goes well for you."

"Do you?"

"Yes, of course. I just want you to be happy."

"I guess I've always known that," she said. "You have meant so much to me."

I put my finger to her lips. "Stop, okay? You don't have to say a thing. Knowing you has been a great experience for me, and I wouldn't trade it for the world. You've taught me so much, so let's just leave it at that, okay?"

She nodded.

We continued walking.

"What will you do now?" she asked.

"Tomorrow I'll drive to Boston and plead my case with the dean of the Harvard Law School. I'm hoping that he'll admit me on a provisional basis for winter term."

"How are you going to pay for law school?" she asked.

"I'll have to take out a student loan."

"Right. Well, good luck."

"Thanks. I'll need it."

Autumn's dad won the election by a 57% to 43% majority. Also, his health continued to improve, so we were both glad about that.

Two days later Autumn and I went our separate ways to an uncertain future.

Chapter Fourteen

"We don't usually make these kinds of exceptions," Dr. Stanton, dean of the Harvard Law School, said after I told him I wanted to be accepted into law school for the spring term that started in January.

"Yes, I'm sure it is unusual." I handed him my resume. "But it's not like I've been wasting my time this semester. I've been serving as an administrative assistant for the mayor of a small town in Illinois." I handed him a list of the duties and responsibilities Autumn and I had while working with her dad. "As you can see, this internship provided me with invaluable training and experience."

He looked over what I'd written.

Next I handed him three letters. "These are letters of recommendation—the first one from the professor of my Contemporary Issues class at Gresham University, the second from my LDS mission president, and the third a letter from the mayor of Scottsburg, Illinois. I think you'll find them all very supportive of my application. All of them have said they would be happy to speak with you."

He took his glasses off and rubbed his eyes before saying, "Let me ask you something. Why do you want to become a lawyer?"

"I want to serve in city or state government, and perhaps one day even serve in the U.S. Congress."

"I'm interested to know why you want to do that when you could make more money working in the private sector."

"The mayor of Scottsburg has been a role model for me. I want to give the kind of service he's been giving for the past several years."

"I see." He continued to look at my resume. "I see you served a mission for your church. How has that impacted your life?"

"It taught me the importance of working hard and the efficacy of prayer."

"Did you pray about this meeting with me?"

"Yes, I did."

"What did you pray for?"

I cleared my throat and paused a few seconds. "That His will be done."

"What if His will is that you go through the regular admission process and begin next fall, like every other first-year student does?"

"I'd certainly understand that decision. But if that does happen, I'll probably look at other universities that would allow me to begin in January. And if I find something that I like, I may not show up here as a student in the fall. So Harvard will have missed a great opportunity to have me as a student. It's a shame, really."

He laughed. "You remind me of myself at your age. All right, we'll let you in for spring term, but you'd better do well, because if you don't, I'll hear about it."

"I won't let you down," I said.

And so the last week of January, I began at Harvard Law School.

It was almost impossible to find a class I could take that didn't have a prerequisite. But for two classes, I talked the instructors into letting me in, even though I was a new student. In retrospect, it was probably a bad decision. I never studied so hard in my life.

Of course, I knew that Autumn was living in Utah, working for Christopher's aunt and no doubt seeing Christopher every day, but the only contact I had from her was on Facebook. I expected to receive a wedding announcement from her any day.

One bleak day the last week in February, she sent me a text message asking me what I was doing.

I told her that I was studying. She asked where. I said the law school library. She asked what floor. I said I was on the third floor. She asked where exactly on the third floor. I told her I was in conference room three.

Strangely enough I was so wrapped up in studying that I didn't wonder why she wanted to know so many details.

Five minutes later someone opened the door, which was behind me. I didn't even turn around.

"What're you doin' in here?" a gruff voice said. "I got this room now. Room three, right?"

I didn't even turn around. "You don't have this room reserved, okay? I do."

"I don't think so! You got some nerve, takin' my room, that's all I gotta say!"

"Great, this is all I need," I muttered. I stood up, but when I turned around, I saw Autumn standing there with a huge grin on her face.

"I so fooled you."

"I knew it was you. I was just playing you."

"No, you totally bought it."

We stood there staring at each other. She wasn't wearing glasses, and her hair looked different. She looked amazing. Of course that depressed me. I figured she'd done it just to please Elder Wonderful.

"You look good," I said somewhat bitterly. "You got contacts, right?"

"Yeah."

"Let me guess—Christopher suggested it, right?"

"It wasn't because of him."

"Yeah, right," I muttered.

That made her mad. "Look, I had some extra money from my job! That's the reason. It had nothing to do with Christopher."

"Okay, if you say so."

I considered hugging her but didn't because, for all I knew, she might be engaged or even married.

"So, what are you doing here?" I asked.

"My aunt lives in Brookline. She's had some health issues so I thought I'd come out here and see if I could help her."

"How's she doing?"

"Better."

"Good. Oh, sorry, do you want to sit down?"

"Thanks," she said and sat across from me. "I brought you some chocolate."

"It's about time. When we were in Penstock's class, I spent so much on chocolate for you that I had to take out a student loan."

"And to think you never had one piece yourself. What a martyr."

"Well, okay, maybe I had one piece."

"Yeah, sure, that's what they all say." She handed me the bag.

I took a piece and put it in my mouth. "Wow, that's actually good."

"I know. I've been sampling it since I picked it up from the Chicago airport."

I took a deep breath because I knew this next part was going to be awkward. "So, how's Christopher?"

"Good I guess, but I haven't seen him for awhile. I broke up with him a couple of weeks ago."

"Sorry."

"I'm not. How are you doing? How's law school?" she asked.

"It's a total disaster."

"In what way?"

"Because I started in January, I don't have any of the prerequisites for most of the classes I'm taking. I need about three more hours a day of study time just to catch up."

"Is there anything I can do to help you while I'm staying here with my aunt?"

I shrugged. "I don't know. Probably not. Thanks for asking though."

"You missed starting fall semester because you were

helping my dad. There must be something I can do. C'mon, we're good at working together. Let's see what we can come up with to give you a little more time to study, okay?"

She asked for a blank sheet of paper and then, like we'd done a hundred times before, she made two columns. Above the left column she wrote *Obstacles,* and above the right column she wrote *Possible Solutions.* Below the first column she wrote *Need more study time.*

"Tell me how your typical day goes," she said.

"I spend four to six hours a day in class, and then the next ten to twelve hours studying. I get about six hours of sleep. Once a week I do laundry. I spend all day Saturday studying. On Sunday I go to church. After church is over, I take a nap. I mostly eat Ramen noodles because it's cheap and fast. That's my life."

"Well, for one thing, I could do your laundry for you."

I shook my head. "I can't have you doing my laundry."

"Why not? I've done my brother's laundry before. What's the big deal?" She wrote down *Do laundry* on the right-hand side of the page.

"I'd feel too self conscious knowing you were doing my laundry. Like I'd have to wash a shirt first so you wouldn't notice I'd spilled food on it."

"I'll tell you what. I'll close my eyes when I put your things in the wash. That way I won't see what's dirty."

I shook my head. "I don't know. Laundry is like . . . well . . . kind of personal."

"How about if we just try it this week? Hopefully it will give you a little more study time."

"You know what? I'm still a little *ambivalent* about the idea."

She stared at me in disbelief.

"Vocabulary.com," I said triumphantly and grinned at her.

"I'm impressed. Look, let's move on. I'm going to do your laundry this week, okay?"

"Okay, but I just want you to know I'll be eating my tacos this week without picante sauce."

"What a martyr," she scoffed. And then she wrote *Bad nutrition* on the left-hand column. "Also, I'm not happy that you're mostly eating Ramen noodles. That alone might be affecting your mental processes. How about if I come in twice next week and cook for you? Like casseroles and things that will last a few days."

"You can't cook," I scoffed.

"What do you mean I can't cook? Of course I can." She paused. "I mean, how hard can it be, right?"

"Why would you waste your time cooking for me?"

She pursed her lips as she tried to gain control of her emotions. She spoke softly. "Because you are my friend. And because you came and rescued my family when we needed help. I will never forget that. Not ever. So, now, let me at least partially repay the favor."

"What about your aunt? You have to take care of her, right?"

"Well, yeah, of course." She cleared her throat. "But she mostly just needs me in the morning. So it'll be okay. How else can I help you?"

I shook my head.

"What's wrong?" she asked.

"You know what? The truth is . . ." It was too embarrassing to say it.

"What? Tell me."

"I'm not sure I even belong here. Day after day I sit in class not understanding anything the professor is saying. I look around at the others in the class, and they're all nodding their heads, like for them it's easy. But it's not easy for me. Nothing is easy for me here."

She reached for my hand.

I hated to let her know how much of a failure I was. "Sometimes, I just want to pack up and go home." I sighed. "The only reason I haven't done that yet is because if I go home, my dad will say he didn't expect I'd make it here anyway."

She came around, stood behind me, and started to massage my shoulders. "My mom does this for my dad when he's had a hard day. Your shoulder muscles are so tight, a person could play a song on 'em like a violin. But I'll fix that."

A few minutes later she asked, "How's that?"

"It's good. Thanks."

She took the piece of paper she'd been using, crumpled it up, and lobbed it into the garbage can near the door. "Autumn—one. Nicolas—zero."

"What?"

"You heard me. I've been practicing. You're toast, my friend."

I couldn't let that stand. We battled it out for the next few minutes. But then in a moment of weakness, I took her in my arms and kissed her. I'd forgotten how amazing that felt. I felt like I'd come home.

A short time later, we broke our embrace. I think we were both a little embarrassed.

"I've missed that so much," I said softly.

"Me too. But not just that. I've missed everything else that went with it."

"Yeah, we had some good times together, didn't we?" I said.

"The best. You want to know what finally ended it with me and Christopher? It was his refusal to play this very game with me. I tossed a paper cup into the garbage can in their kitchen and said, 'Autumn—one, Christopher—zero.' And he frowned at me and told me to stop being immature. And so I'm thinking, 'Where does he get off telling me I'm immature?' That's when I decided I *wanted* to be immature my whole life. And who else could I do that with but you?" She laughed because she knew what my reaction would be.

"Uh, could we tweak that just a little?" I asked. "Maybe replace *immature* with *playful?*"

"You know we're not going to issue a press release after this, right?"

"Yeah."

"C'mon, Nicky-boy, let me cheer you up while I'm here. Let me make you laugh. It's the least I can do after all you did for my dad."

"Well, I admit, if anyone could cheer me up here, it's you. But, you know what? I'll be in law school for another three years. And I doubt your aunt is going to need you that long."

"Probably not." She touched her chin as if she was in deep thought. "Hmmm, there must be some . . . I don't know . . . some other arrangement we could come up with for a more long-term association together."

I shrugged. "I don't know what it would be."

"Well, think about it, okay? You're clever. I'm sure you'll come up with something." And then she gave me that silly grin of hers, the one I'd first seen when I had been chasing her through the park, the day we first kissed.

We stopped talking and just stared into each other's eyes.

I can't believe this, I thought to myself. *She's here! She came to see me. She's everything I've ever wanted, the only girl I've ever loved. It probably doesn't much matter if I make it through law school or not. But if we're together, I can't imagine not being happy, no matter what happens.*

She was still smiling at me, waiting, I suppose, for me to say the obvious.

I cleared my throat nervously. "Well, of course, uh, and I know this might be totally inappropriate to say, what with you so recently having ended a relationship, and I would guess that you probably need time to work through all those, you know, issues and such, so I can understand if this isn't what you had in mind . . ."

"Yes?" she said, her eyes open wide.

"Well, I was just thinking—and I know this sounds crazy—but there's always the possibility that we could, uh, you know . . . get married."

"Marriage? Hmmm." She tapped her index finger on her lips. "What an interesting idea. Maybe we should consider that. Do you have some more paper?"

On another sheet of paper she wrote *Reasons to Get Married.* "I guess the first thing we need to resolve is if we even love each other," she said.

"I'm in," I said quickly.

"You sure?"

"Are you kidding? I fell in love with you by the second week of Penstock's class. I didn't say anything, though, because all you could talk about was Christopher. I was afraid that if I pushed it, you'd quit seeing me."

"For me it didn't happen right away. At first I was mainly blown away that we worked so well together. So first I admired you. But when I was in Utah, I started comparing you with Christopher. That's when I finally realized how truly amazing you are. So I'm happy to say now that I love you with all my heart."

She wrote *We love each other.*

"That's a good start," I said.

"Yeah, for sure. What other reasons should we put down about why we should get married?" she asked.

"How about this? We both honor our baptismal and temple covenants."

"Excellent." She wrote that down.

"I've got another one," she said. "How about this?" She wrote down *Problem-solving skills.* And then she said, "True or false? Life is mostly filled with challenges and problems to be solved."

"True."

She paused. "Don't take this wrong, okay? But I think I could be happily married to any worthy guy who honored his priesthood. Especially if we had enough money, he had a good job, our kids were healthy, we were living gospel principles, and we prayed together as a family and as a couple. But problems happen. And that's where you and I have an advantage. We've been working together solving problems since we first met each other."

"We have."

"What if the only thing we'd ever done together is watch movies and make out?" she asked.

I couldn't resist appearing clueless. "You're saying that would have been a bad thing?"

She crumpled up the first sheet of paper we'd used and lobbed it in my direction.

I nodded. "I got it. I got it. Making out all the time and watching movies wouldn't be enough preparation for the challenges of married life."

"That's it."

"This whole thing is a little intimidating," I said. "I mean being married. Mortgages, kids—the whole package."

"A little. But, of course, there will be good times, too. For example, if we do get married, it would be nice if you came home for lunch once in a while."

I shrugged. "Yeah, sure, why not?"

"When you do, I'll be ready for you." She gave me a look I'd never seen before.

"You mean like you'll have made some sandwiches?"

"Listen very carefully." She said it very slowly. "I . . . personally . . . will be ready for you."

I got it, okay? But I couldn't resist dragging it out. "Home-made soup on a cold day is always tasty," I said.

Clearly I was making her crazy. "Look, I'm not talking about some stupid soup. Okay?" she complained.

"Oh, right . . . you mean *lunch*."

This was new territory for both of us.

"You think that might brighten your day?" she asked with a big grin on her face.

"Oh yeah, definitely!"

She nodded. "Mine, too, actually."

I grinned. "Well, okay then, let's get married!"

"Let's do! When would be the best time for you to get married?" she asked.

"Are you serious? I'd say tonight or, at the latest, tomorrow!"

She laughed. "I didn't mean convenient for *you*! I meant convenient for our families!"

"Oh, *that* kind of convenient," I grumbled. "All right, let's give 'em like two weeks."

"My mom and I won't be able to make all the preparations for a reception in two weeks. You know, like the cake, reserving a place, things like that."

"You think I care about any of that?" I asked.

"No, I'm sure you don't, but it'll be important to my mom."

I reached for my Blackberry. "Let me see what holidays are coming up."

A minute later I had it. "My spring break runs from March 14 to March 18. So we could get married on Saturday, the 12th, and I wouldn't have to be back to school until Monday, the 21st. How does that sound?"

"March 12th isn't that far away. I don't know if that'll be enough time."

"We can do it. We'll make the arrangements, take the pictures, do the invitations, and we'll be done in a day or two—tops."

We spent the next hour working on details. We agreed to get married on March 12th. We chose the Chicago Temple because it was close to both our families.

"Out of respect for your dad, I'd like to call him and ask his permission to marry you," I said.

"That's a great idea! He'll be pleased to hear from you. He always has such great things to say about you."

"I'll call him tomorrow morning."

"Good. I won't talk to my folks until after you've talked to him."

"So are we basically engaged?" I asked as we were leaving conference room three.

"Well, let's talk about that, okay? Some day our kids are going to ask about how we became engaged," she said. "I'd like to tell them how you gave me a rose, got down on your knees, and proposed to me in some romantic place. Will you do that for me?"

"I'd be honored to propose to you. How about tomorrow night, after I talk to your dad?"

"Okay, thank you."

"Could you do me a favor and act surprised when I propose?" I asked.

"I will. I promise."

Just before we left the library, she stopped me. "How are you and your dad getting along?" she asked.

"Great. He doesn't contact me, and I don't contact him."

"You've got to make peace with him before we get married. I don't want any tension between the two of you in the temple."

"What do you suggest I do?" I asked.

"Call him and apologize."

"For what?"

"For thinking that his not being willing to pay your way through law school meant he didn't love you anymore."

"I don't know if I can do that."

"I'm sure you can. If you need any help planning out what you're going to say, let me know."

"I'll think about it, okay?"

"Okay."

Once we were outside on the steps of the library, Autumn shouted to the entire world. "Look at us, everybody! We're off on another adventure! Just like in *Scooby-Doo!*"

I groaned and looked around, hoping nobody had heard her. "Uh, here at Harvard, we don't usually talk much about *Scooby-Doo*."

"Well, you should."

"You want to come and see my apartment?" I asked.

"Is it clean?" she teased.

"No, not really."

"I'll pass. Besides, we're nearly engaged now, so we need to be careful. I should get back to my aunt's place."

"Let me come with you. I'd like to meet your aunt and see how she's doing."

That got her flustered. "Uh . . . she might not be home yet."

"Where is she?"

She took a deep breath. "Well, actually, she went . . . uh . . . bowling with some friends."

"Well, that's good therapy. So, she must be doing a lot better then, right?"

"Yes, she is. Thanks for asking."

We took a few more steps, and then she stopped me. "Look, this isn't right! I can't start out our life together with a lie. The truth is, my aunt's not that sick."

"How sick is she?"

Big sigh. "She's not sick at all. I didn't come to Boston

for her. I came to see how you were doing and to see if there was any hope for us."

I laughed.

"What? I needed an excuse so if you didn't want to have anything to do with me, I could find out and go home without looking totally pathetic."

"I'm so glad you came. I've been miserable here without you."

"You want to know what made the difference? I was telling my dad that I was thinking of changing my Facebook status so you'd know I'd broken up with Christopher, and he said, 'Are you crazy? You're going to trust this to Facebook? Listen to me! You get yourself on a plane, and you fly out there, and you talk to Nick! That boy's worth it!'"

I laughed again. "I hope he's right."

"He is."

A few minutes later, there we were, two people waiting for a subway. We might have been mistaken for lifelong residents of Boston except that Autumn kept looking down the track to see if the subway was coming.

"Do you have any more paper on you?" she asked.

"Yeah, sure. Why do you ask?"

"We probably should talk about finances."

"Not much to talk about. I'm a hundred percent on student loans."

"Maybe I could get a job here to help out."

"That'd be great. Okay, we'll talk about that," I said.

"And, you know, we should also talk about having a family."

"Right. We'll talk about that too. We'll have a great future together."

"Also, while I'm here, can we go to the temple?" she asked.

"Good idea."

She was looking down the track. "Oh, look, here it comes!"

"Can I ask you a question?" I asked. "You're not going to make me watch *Scooby-Doo* on our honeymoon, are you?"

She smiled. "We'll be too busy for that."

Big grin on my face. "I like being busy."

We were married as planned, on March 12th, and that was only the beginning of the many adventures Autumn and I have had since that day, and will have through the rest of our lives together, and actually, beyond that.

About the Author

Jack Weyland has long-since secured his place as the foremost LDS young adult novelist. The author of some twenty-seven bestselling books, he has entertained and inspired generations of readers. After his retirement as a professor of physics at BYU–Idaho, he and his wife, Sherry, served a full-time mission in Long Island, New York. The Weylands have five children and sixteen grandchildren; they reside in Rexburg, Idaho.